POWER
Play

Nan Comargue

CRIMSON
ROMANCE
F+W Media, Inc.

Published by
Crimson Romance
an imprint of F+W Media, Inc.
10151 Carver Road, Suite 200
Blue Ash, Ohio 45242

www.crimsonromance.com

ISBN 10: 1-4405-5880-9
ISBN 13: 978-1-4405-5880-1
eISBN 10: 1-4405-5879-5
eISBN 13: 978-1-4405-5879-5

Chapter One

Under the bright crisp lights of the arena, Lila leaned forward to watch the figures slide by. The ice surface was littered with twirling figure skaters and ice dancing pairs. She paid these skaters no attention. Her velvet brown eyes were riveted to the lumbering forms of the hockey players.

Between the other more graceful figures, the players skated with power and intensity. Even in this informal atmosphere, their concentration was palpable. All energies were given to their stride and the warm-up exercises that preceded the actual practice.

Lila knew from a lifetime of experience that the ice surface would soon be cleared. Though the professional hockey players sometimes used this local arena for their practices, it did not mean they would deign to share the space with amateurs. The figure skaters, the ice dancers, and the simple pleasure skaters would have to leave in a half hour. In the meantime, several of the mere mortals took the opportunity to sidle up to their favorite hockey star and demand an autograph. A few of the players obliged.

Lost in her scrutiny, Lila did not notice the man coming up behind her until he laid a hand on her shoulder.

Startled, she spun around to confront him. It was only upon spying the familiar smiling face that her own face lost its look of habitual wariness.

"Sorry I'm late," the newcomer apologized, his breath coming in convincing pants. "I had to sprint to avoid the media types."

Though she had an uneasy suspicion why the media might be chasing him, she refrained from making a comment. Instead, she smiled to show her lack of disgruntlement. She was, in fact, early for their assignation.

Her companion hitched his heavy nylon bag further up his shoulder. "Are you sure you want to stay for the practice? It's not exactly fun to watch."

"I know," she said.

Jack Jarrett's pale blue eyes skittered away. He remembered why she was so familiar with the lives of professional hockey players.

"Has he shown up yet?" Jack's dark head jerked to indicate the ice surface.

"No, but I haven't been watching." She shrugged a slender shoulder. "Maybe he won't show."

"He will," her companion predicted.

Almost against her inclination, Lila found herself trying to persuade him. "He was traded only yesterday, Jack. I mean, he wouldn't be expected to play today, much less attend practice."

Jack's jaw flexed. "He will. He'll want to show his new teammates that he's just one of the guys, that he's not too good to go to practice like the rest of them, even if it's an optional one. He may be a superstar, darling, but he's probably the most well-liked player in the league."

No one who knew Jack as well as Lila could mistake the bitterness in his voice. It colored his usually mellow tenor tones, distorting the pleasant features that had first drawn her to him. After Cahal she had promised herself that she would never again become involved with a sports figure. She'd broken that rule in the first few months after the separation.

"Perhaps," Lila said, "I should go."

Her companion's eyes softened as they lingered on her upturned face. Jack was six foot one while Lila was only a few inches above five feet in height. Even so, the height difference was more manageable than it had been with her husband. Her former husband, Lila corrected herself. The divorce was only a matter of formality.

"No, darling. I want you to stay." His face tightened. "Why should we change the plans we made days ago just because Cahal

Wallace is coming here? Other players' girlfriends watch the practices sometimes."

She liked the confidence with which he made the statement. Theirs had been rather a whirlwind romance but that did not, in Lila's opinion, make it any less valid. She and Cahal had known each other for years before they got married. Familiarity and time were not buttresses against betrayal and pain.

Lila reached for his hand. "I know, Jack."

Still holding hands, the couple sauntered away from the ice, moving into the hallway.

"I have to get ready," he said. "I'm late as it is. Watch for me on the ice, okay?"

Watching his tall figure disappear up the hallway to the dressing room, Lila wondered who he supposed she was going to watch for if it wasn't him.

She made her way back down the hall. Amid those bodies hustling away from the arena now that the rink was closed to the public and those making their way to the dressing room to suit up, Lila's scarlet-clad figure was incongruous. Her sweater, her scarf, and her pea coat were all crimson. Only her long slim skirt was a less vivid gray. The bright colors played well against her black hair and her dark olive complexion.

Even in multicultural Toronto, few strangers were able to identify her ethnic background with any degree of success. The suggestions ranged from Spanish to Italian, from Brazilian to Indian—both of the East Indian and Native Canadian varieties. The confusion no doubt arose from the fact that Lila's father had been a Russian sailor and her mother a West Indian from an Indian background.

She had never known either of her parents. Raised by her maternal grandparents in Toronto, she had lived with them until she married at the age of twenty-two. They had both been dead for over five years.

Except for Jack, she was remarkably alone. That was, she readily admitted to herself, one of the reasons Jack was in her life in the first place. She could stand to be alone for now but the thought of the days stretching into months and years terrified her. Loneliness she could only take in small doses.

The nearby commotion alerted her to the long-awaited arrival. Cahal Wallace. Toronto's new goaltender. The man of the hour.

Unable to resist observing, Lila watched as a group of three men entered the doors to her left. There were, unexpectedly, no reporters with them. These were quite obviously three hockey players. She would have known that even if she had not recognized them.

Lila turned her attention back to the ice surface, which was filling up with players in their bright practice uniforms as well as an assistant coach carrying a clipboard. The players made lazy circles around the rink, their careful strides eating up the distance between the encircling boards.

It was clear that she had been spotted when the conversation between the three men fell silent. She imagined that she could feel a pair of very clear, very piercing gray eyes focused on her back.

"Lila?"

There was a huskiness in his voice that had nothing to do with his emotions, if indeed he was feeling any at this impromptu reunion. That low rasp was his natural speaking tone.

She took several seconds to turn to face him. The other men had halted on either side but she took no notice of them. It was his figure toward which all eyes were drawn, tall and blond and muscular.

Lila took the time to force a smile.

"Hello, Cahal. How do you like being back in Toronto?"

Like her, he had been raised in this city.

"I was here a few months ago," he said.

She knew. He had called and called at her house. She still didn't know how he got her number. After two days, he had been gone again. His team had chalked up a victory in Toronto.

Cahal Wallace was one of the league's most consistent goaltenders. Just forty-eight hours before, the entire population of Toronto had despised him for his mental toughness and his fluid range of movement. Now they were prepared to adore him if he could bring his winning record to their city.

"I thought," he went on, "you were never going to set foot in a hockey arena again as long as you lived."

Her foolish words came back to haunt her. Nearly a year ago, the last time they had spoken, she'd thrown those words at him with all of the hurt and loathing she had carried in her agonized heart. Now she wondered how she could have been so melodramatic. Divorce, after all, was not exactly the stuff of fairy tales. They happened all the time. They happened to hockey players, they happened to high school sweethearts, they happened to her.

The two men flanking her former husband looked embarrassed to be witnessing the exchange. Despite Cahal's low reasonable voice, there was something personal about the conversation. And, Lila suspected, these two Toronto players knew more about her presence at the arena today than Cahal did.

Lila's sense of fair play demanded that she warn him. It would be worse if he learned the truth through their divorce lawyers or from an unsubtle newspaper headline.

She considered requesting a private moment with him; however, she shied away from spending any time alone. She was afraid of what those daring gray eyes might persuade her to do.

"I'm here to watch Jack Jarrett practice. We're dating."

She had the unsatisfying pleasure of seeing him flinch. Having expected to be more happy to see him hurt in this way, Lila was disappointed.

"Jack Jarrett?" Her husband repeated the name after a moment's pause. "He's the seventh defenseman, isn't he?"

Lila had no cause to be upset at this accurate assessment of Jack's skill. He was indeed the seventh defenseman in Toronto, the man who was called upon to play when one of the six regular defensemen was injured or scratched from the lineup. Jack knew, she hoped, exactly where he stood on the team and in the league. Though he was, at thirty, in the prime of his career, he was fortunate to be in a job at present.

Cahal fixed her with a penetrating stare. "How long has this been going on?"

The implication was obvious but Lila didn't rise to the bait.

"None of your business," she said, smiling all the while.

Her husband, too, smiled, giving her the benefit of straight, utterly false, white teeth.

"I wouldn't make plans for an engagement, darling."

The smile, as much as the menacing tone, caused her to shiver.

"Don't try to intimidate me," she told him, afraid that the success of his tactic was already evident in her wavering voice.

"I'm not. I'm just offering you a piece of advice. Don't plan for an engagement because it won't take place. And while you're at it, I'd suggest that you not make any big plans to celebrate the divorce."

Oddly enough, the last threat made Lila relax. She knew that nothing could stop the divorce proceedings. In another month, the year measured out since their final separation would have expired and she would be free. Nothing Cahal could do would alter that.

She almost opened her mouth to tell him this but he was already moving away, apparently content with what he had already said. If only Lila were not left with the firm idea that her ex-husband had gotten the best of the conversation.

*

As it turned out, Jack Jarrett didn't play a big part in the practice. He wasn't expected to play in the game that night.

It was just as well that Jack did not skate much as Lila was unable to focus on anyone other than the man in the stark black goalie mask. Cahal had not had the time to repaint his mask since learning of his trade, and rather than wear the colors of his former team he would be playing that night in unrelieved black.

It had been years since she had watched Cahal play, still longer since she had seen him do so in person. He was a blur of movement. Flexible, graceful, fluid. He anticipated nearly every puck that came in his direction. Those he did not anticipate, he twisted and lunged at impossible angles in order to deter. He was intimidating in the net; at six feet four inches, he was by any account a tall goaltender. He seemed to fill every possible open space, allowing for little leeway to oncoming players.

He was beautiful to watch. A wonderful marriage of strength and flexibility.

It was, Lila told herself, perfectly possible to admire a man without feeling anything for him. Even if that man was one to whom she had been married for nearly six years.

In spite of her avowed apathy, she was glad to see the ice surface empty and the men move back toward the dressing rooms. Practice was over and she would not have to face Cahal again. Perhaps never again.

Jack was one of the first players out of the locker room. Once they moved together toward the entrance of the arena, however, the two of them were swamped by bodies.

Some of the amassed crowd were merely autograph seekers hunting the latest Toronto acquisition. A goodly minority, however, were the journalists Lila had been hoping to avoid.

The shouting started as soon as her face became clear. Jack's body could not hide her very well.

"Mrs. Wallace! Mrs. Wallace!"

Other reporters were more familiar. "Lila! Over here! Lila!"

Photographers snapped her picture, her face still half-obscured by Jack's shielding figure.

None of the reporters were waiting for her to answer. They continued to shout their questions at her and Jack's retreating figures.

"How does it feel to have your husband here in Toronto?"

"When's the divorce, Lila?"

"Any plans for a wedding?"

It was only the steadiness of Jack's hand over hers that kept her from sprinting to the car. That would have made a funny shot, her hair and scarf flying out behind her as she made like an Olympic athlete.

She hated to be made to look silly almost as much as she hated feeling so hunted by the press. The attempts at contact had been pretty constant since her relationship with Jack had been made public. Cahal's superstar status, combined with the fact that his romantic rival was a fellow hockey player, had made an irresistible human interest piece. Sports fans ate up the innuendo as eagerly as soap opera fans might have done.

"God, I hate this," Jack muttered, slipping into the driver's seat of his sports car. With his aid, Lila was already seated in the passenger seat.

Lila looked at him, alerted by something in his tone. "Have they been hounding you a lot?"

Her companion nodded as he swung the car out of the parking space. "The reporters know that the divorce is coming up. We are local celebrities, you know."

Lila, who considered herself a private citizen, did not appreciate this piece of news. She could understand how athletes attracted fame but she was not an athlete, she merely had the misfortune to have been married to one. And now she was dating another. Perhaps the press felt that she deserved to be hounded if only for her unfortunate choices in partners.

"The reporters loved Cahal and me," she said, leaning her head back against the plush seat. "Our marriage made a good story, good publicity. High school sweethearts, childhood friends and all that. By the time we were married, Cahal was already the number one goalie in Chicago, already a star. Marrying the hometown girl was a good career move. I am sure that it sold a few more jerseys."

Jack looked sideways at her but he said nothing. Probably, he had never heard that ugly note in her voice before. Lila hated to hear it.

"I'm sorry, Jack." She felt she ought to apologize for that tone, if not the words themselves. "There is so much history between Cahal and me. I think I hate that most of all."

"That's understandable," he replied. "Now it must feel as if you wasted so much time. He was the first guy you dated, wasn't he?"

"Yes. The only one."

"I know you knew each other since childhood," Jack went on. "How old were you when you first met?"

It seemed odd to be raising the question now but Lila was unable to see the strangeness of the situation. Seeing the man must naturally bring up questions concerning him.

"We were six," she said, smiling because she knew the entire story by heart. The times he had been traveling on the road, or playing on a different junior hockey team, she had repeated this story to herself like a nursery rhyme.

"We were in grade one at the time. Cahal had just moved to Toronto from Sudbury because his parents wanted him to have the best coaches and teams to play on. Even then, they had known that he was something special, a talented player. Anyway, we met in Mrs. Vaughn's class that year and spent about ten more years in the same classes, more or less ignoring one another like boys and girls do at that age."

That was not entirely true, of course. She had been unable to ignore him completely. Cahal Wallace was the little boy whom all the little girls had a crush on at one time or another. Lila had suffered through three of her own friends liking him. At the time, she had not seen the attraction. She had had fleeting crushes of her own, on Ricky Deen and Jesse Fernandez.

"I never even noticed Cahal during all those years," she continued, "except to know that he was sort of famous for playing hockey. Even then he was getting a great deal of attention. Then, when we were fourteen, in the first year of high school, he asked me to dance at the Valentine's Day dance. All throughout grades nine and ten, we danced at the dances and we became pretty good friends."

Abruptly, her narrative broke off. She was coming to the part of the story that she loved best, and that her mind had recently begun to gloss over. The memories of those sweet first days were not the kind of recollections she wanted any longer. It stung her that they could still resurface and with such force.

"And then?" her companion prompted. He sounded an echo of her own thoughts.

And then what, Lila? And then, he gave you the happiest days of your life.

"In grade eleven," she said, "he was traded to a junior hockey team up in northern Ontario. He had to move away from his parents, his friends, his school. Everything had to change."

"I know about that," Jack said. "I was traded a couple times in juniors."

Lila paid this information no attention.

"He could only come back about once a month, and during the end of the school year and into the summers. When he did finally come back, it was hard to fit in. His friends had changed, the schoolwork was different. His parents were going through their separation around that time. Cahal was trying to keep them all together by playing as best as he could, studying for hours every night so that his playing would not affect his grades."

Jack grimaced. "But he found time for you, didn't he? In the middle of all that playing and studying, he managed to keep in touch with you, right?"

Lila was thinking of that first letter from him after he had gone up north. It had been five pages long and she still had it, preserved between the pages of a childhood book.

In between the lines of that letter, he had told her how much he had loved her. There had been no talk of love, of course. Not at sixteen or even at seventeen, but they had both known during those years. There had been a tacit agreement that Lila would not date any of the Toronto boys who asked her out and that Cahal would not look too hard at the girls at his new high school.

Their summers had been almost devoted to one another. They saw every new movie and listened to every new CD. They had held hands and kissed and groped a little in the back of his car. In those last three years of high school, Lila did not remember a single argument between the two of them.

"We wrote each other," Lila answered. "And he came home as often as he could. By the time we were seventeen, we were boyfriend and girlfriend. Then, of course, he was drafted."

"Third overall draft choice," said Jack, who had been drafted one hundred and thirty-fourth.

"He went to Chicago and I stayed here. I wanted to go to university and get my degree, that had been my grandparents' dream. Then, I finished my bachelor's degree in English—"

"And the superstar Chicago goaltender came back to marry you," her companion finished. His hands were tight on the steering wheel. "How simple."

Looking back, it had been simple. Cahal had made it so. The first contract he had signed as a professional hockey player had made him a millionaire. He bought modest houses and cars for his parents, then divorced from each other, and bought himself a flashier German sports car. He had been content to rent an apartment in Chicago at that time. Together, they had bought their first house and he had wanted it to be his first home as well so he had waited for her.

"He paid for my university studies," Lila said. She had never told anyone that before and she said it now as if confessing a sin.

Jack turned to look at her and she met his gaze.

"My grandparents might have managed to pay for university," she said, "but on their income that would have meant putting a mortgage on the house and that house was all that they really had. They would have done it, too, but when Cahal offered the money it was like a godsend."

"So you took it." There was a note of honest shock in Jack's voice. She knew that this revelation jarred with his idea of her, the idea she had constructed for him of herself as a firmly independent woman. The truth was that her means had always come from Cahal.

"Rather than shackling my elderly grandparents with a mortgage? Yes, I took the money. If he had offered it differently, if his parents had objected even in the slightest, perhaps I would not have done it. But I did, because Cahal acted like it was the simplest thing in the world. He had the money and I did not. Rather than take out a mortgage on the house, which still meant that I would have had to work part-time and during the summers, I took the money. Not borrowed it. Took it."

"But you paid him back, didn't you?" Jack's voice was tight, as if it were being stretched on the rack.

Lila was angry. "I didn't marry him as a kind of repayment, if that's what you mean."

"No? But it must have been a lot of money. Twenty or thirty thousand at least."

"It was almost a selfish act on his part," Lila heard herself justifying. "If I had had to work during the summers, that would have meant seeing almost nothing of one another during those years. Paying for my tuition meant that he could have all of my time during the summer time or whenever he was in town."

Somehow that still made it sound as if Cahal had purchased her. It had been nothing of the sort. It had been natural, almost inevitable, at the time. Cahal had been as proud of her studying as her grandparents. Maybe more so. His career had made it so that he couldn't attend university.

"Well, you kept a home for him for six years," Jack acceded. "It's not as if you owe him for whatever he might have spent on your studies. A few thousand dollars is hardly a drain for a man who makes, what, six or seven million a year. More than that now, I guess."

Lila knew exactly how much Cahal Wallace made; it was set out in the divorce papers. And it was substantially more than six million. She imagined Jack was pretending not to know the exact figure. Cahal's salary in Chicago had been publicized.

Whatever the figure, Jack was right. Her tuition had hardly been a drain on his resources, even so many years ago. The drain, if any, was in the form of Cahal's alcoholic mother and his father who now had three young children from his second marriage. Both older Wallaces had sacrificed in their early years to provide their son with the best of opportunities. In later years, they had come to remind Cahal of this fact at increasingly frequent intervals.

She said nothing of this to Jack because it was none of his business. Cahal's personal life was just that, personal. The truth about her tuition and her degree was her own secret to tell. The truth about her marriage was another secret and someday, though she could not picture the occasion, she would feel comfortable enough with someone to share it. Someday.

Chapter Two

Lila was tired by the end of the day, though she had done nothing of any merit. She had eaten lunch with Jack, making strained conversation and trying to avoid the gazes of the other diners. She came home and watched television for a while, had been depressed by the news, and finally settled down to reread one of her old books.

She knew very well the reason for her fatigue and it had everything to do with her husband. Her ex-husband, though Cahal no doubt would have denied that label.

How odd it was that he should be behaving in such a way now after all the time that had passed since the separation. Acting as if she were pig-headedly pursuing a divorce for the sake of capriciousness, as if she did not have very good reasons.

Perhaps, Lila reasoned, Cahal had simply been putting on a show for his new teammates. It appeased masculine pride to make a show of possessiveness and that was certainly what he had done. He had marked her as his own, even knowing that another man had a better claim to her nowadays.

But did Jack have any better a claim?

She had known Cahal most of her life and Jack only for a few months. Cahal had sometimes understood her better than she herself while Jack seemed to be in perpetual confusion regarding her motivations.

Admittedly, she had chosen Jack to be a contrast to her first husband and he was in everything except his career. Even that was not so terrible seeing as Jack worked most of the time in Toronto, just as she did. Chicago had been pleasant but it had never been her home.

The irony was that Cahal now lived in Toronto as well. In light of that fact, the arguments they had had in Chicago seemed stupid and pointless. Even then...well, Lila was willing to admit the arguments might have been pointless even at the time. As Cahal had told her a thousand times over, he could not help where he lived. That was simply a function of his job. Countless other careers possessed the same drawbacks.

But it hadn't been just the locale Lila had resented. She had shied away from the celebrity Cahal's talents brought him, the legions of fans who recognized him even in the most faraway places. She hated knowing that he was not just being kind to the fans but that he was happy to sign autographs, to listen to their opinions on the team's chances, to pose for a photograph. He accepted it as a part of his job, as integral as the time on the ice, and he had grown used to the notoriety.

Lila had hated, too, the things he had been unable to change. Cahal could have snubbed the autograph seekers but he was unable to keep his face out of the newspaper when he played hockey games three or four times a week.

She had resented the danger inherent in his playing hockey, the inevitable minor injuries that might one day become career-ending. The muscle strains, the groin pulls, the more routine stiffness or soreness. Occasionally during the playoffs, he might not sleep through the night because of pain.

She had resented never being able to hold down a job because any work she might find would have conflicted with his own unusual hours. Resented being away from her friends so that she was denied even that small way to spend her time. Instead, she joined the Wives and Girlfriends' club in Chicago, joining other players' wives and partners in organizing charity and social events. She would rather have been around when her grandparents had died, would have rather spent that time by their sides.

There was no point in blaming Cahal. He could have insisted

that she marry him right after high school, refusing to put her through university, refusing to allow her those four precious years with her grandparents while she had attended school. Those four years had been years he had spent alone in Chicago.

In the privacy of her small apartment, Lila's nutmeg-colored eyes darkened.

No, she did not imagine that Cahal had been alone all of those years. Along with fans, there were always hockey groupies, young women who were eager to get closer to their favorite player in whatever way they could. Young and handsome and a rising star to boot, Cahal must have had his pick of young beauties while Lila remained innocent, waiting for him in Toronto.

The color came to her pale cheeks as she remembered just how innocent she had been on their wedding night and how surprised that Cahal seemed to know exactly what to do to bring them both pleasure. At the time, like a silly fool, she had thought that such things came instinctively to men. She had not imagined that while she had wanted to save herself for him alone, her new husband might have acquired some experience along the way.

No, Lila told herself, she would not allow her thoughts to take her back to those times. For months she had brooded on the past, searching her memory for any prior signs of her husband's true nature.

In retrospect, she had found it only too easy to find significant clues. Only, after such a long time, she no longer knew if she could trust her memories to be accurate or trust herself not to blur those recollections with her own anger and hurt.

Well, she could not stop herself from having been angry and hurt by Cahal. There was nothing she could do about the past. But there was no way that she would be hurt again. Not by Cahal and not by any man.

*

Monday nights were the usual time for meetings of the Toronto Wives and Girlfriends' club. A reluctant Lila had been urged by her new boyfriend to join two months before. Now she found it a pleasant way to occupy her time.

The other women were cheerful and interesting, and the charity events they planned were useful rather than being decorative social affairs. Last year, Lila learned, the Wives had raised almost half a million dollars for a local children's organization. This year they were planning the same sort of outcome for an earthquake relief fund.

This Monday, however, Lila felt a faint shimmer of apprehension as she arrived at the home of Catherine and Edward Monahan.

Although the meeting times of the Wives were set, the location often varied according to the women's whims and inclinations. Sometimes the rotation occurred every week, with a different woman hosting the club each Monday. Other times one woman would host for weeks on end, taking the pressure off the other families.

At first Lila had felt like an interloper. The majority of the women were actually wives of the players, not merely girlfriends. Lila had wondered whether her status as Jack's girlfriend would give her a diminished role in the club. She had not wondered for long.

The women had been inviting and welcoming. They could well afford to be. Some of the wives had been in Toronto for a dozen or more years. Most had been there for at least a couple of years. Of the three girlfriends who attended, two had been going steady with their boyfriends for several years and the other for at least a year.

Lila's apprehension was that she was now going to be cast in a role she had avoided discussing—that of Cahal Wallace's wife. But tonight was also the first time she was going to attend a Wives meeting without seeing the face of Jessica Gerard, the wife of Toronto's previous goaltender. Jessica had been well liked and respected amongst the Wives. This was the first time that one of the Wives had left for the sake of another's estranged husband.

*

She could feel the tension the moment she stepped into Cathy Monahan's decorated home. Her hostess's smile was polite in the extreme but it was patently false, an exaggerated attempt at friendliness.

This was worse than Lila had anticipated, worse even than she had feared.

Cathy Monahan led Lila toward the living room where she saw that she was among the last to arrive. There were already more than a dozen women in the room, comprising most of the membership of the Toronto Wives and Girlfriends.

Most of the women were dressed more casually than Lila, wearing the slacks, pullovers and blouses that branded them as mothers of small children. Nadia Ivanov had been a gymnast before she had married and Cathy Monahan had been a model but other than that, none of the women worked or desired to do so. Being the wife of a hockey player and mother to children of an often-absent father was a demanding occupation.

Lila felt out of place in her tailored work clothes. There was never any time to change after work.

Ignoring the strain that she felt, Lila greeted the other women, trying not to show any of her discomfort in her posture or her tone.

Unfortunately, the other women had known her for too many weeks to be deterred by a straight backbone or mild tones.

"Ethan told me that you've seen our new goalie," one of the women remarked almost immediately after pleasantries had been exchanged. Ethan was her husband. "What's he like, Lila? It's so hard for a man to tell you what you want to know."

Lila held her breath. Was it possible that they did not know? Could the tension that she had perceived be attributed merely to the fact of Jessica Gerard's husband being traded away from the team?

"I've seen his picture on television," Nadia offered, "but that didn't give me any impression of the man."

Lila's hostess turned cornflower blue eyes upon her. "Yes, Lila, tell us what our newest arrival is like. Eddie told me that you had spoken to him yesterday at practice."

"Forget that," Nadia said. "What does the man look like in the flesh? He is absolutely gorgeous on TV."

There were enthusiastic murmurs of agreement this time, even from women who had attractive husbands of their own waiting at home.

"Well," Lila said, wanting to defer any further prompting, "he's about six foot four, blond, gray eyes, with broad shoulders and a long dimple in one of his cheeks which is hard to see unless he laughs. He has a deep voice, sort of hoarse and raspy."

Another woman immediately interjected. "You can do better than that, Lila, being his wife and all. I don't care how he plays on the ice. What's he like in bed?"

Lila went silent. Since none of the other women had ever lived in Chicago or mentioned Cahal, she hadn't realized that they knew about her marriage. After all, the Wives knew her by her grandparents' name of Ramlall.

Now she saw how naïve she had been. Of course the other women didn't have to know Cahal personally to have read the sport pages or seen her picture on the Internet.

Before she could speak, the doorbell chimed again and Cathy Monahan ran to answer it.

Cathy brought back a woman Lila did not know, a slender blonde. At first Lila assumed it to be one of the Wives who had not attended the meetings for the past few months, who had perhaps been away or having a baby, but the way the conversations all halted when Cathy returned told her that this was not a woman with whom the other Wives were acquainted.

"Ladies," Cathy announced, her excitement suppressed, "may I present Victoria Brantford, Cahal Wallace's significant other."

Lila's first reaction was one of total shock, but that soon gave way to a feeling of all-encompassing relief. She was spared the need to explain her relationship to Cahal, just as she would be in the future spared the questions that would inevitably result from their having had a relationship together. It would be Victoria Brantford who would receive all of the questions, who would have to appease the curiosity about the newest Toronto player.

Victoria was soon settled into a chair by the door where Lila couldn't see her. Even before Cathy could begin the necessary introductions, the new arrival was peppered with questions. How was she doing after the flight over from Chicago? How did she feel about the trade? Had she ever been to Canada before?

They were all polite questions, perfectly reasonable, though they came swift and sure from all corners of the room.

Lila could afford to take pity on the girl, remembering how she had been subject to a similarly well-mannered interrogation upon joining the Wives and Girlfriends. The women were curious, and added to that the superstar status of Cahal Wallace, Victoria was sure to attract some attention.

Lila remained in the background, sipping on the soft drink that the Monahan's maid had given to her. From her distant vantage point, she couldn't see the newcomer. She could just make out the clear confident answers that the new arrival made to the questions the other Wives were throwing at her.

How closed-mouthed Cahal had been the previous day. He had virtually forbidden her remarriage yet he had had a girlfriend tucked up his sleeve. A year ago, she would not have believed him capable of such casual deception. She was a great deal wiser today.

Finally, the other women's inquiries being exhausted, Cathy Monahan was able to perform her function as hostess and introduce the other women to the newcomer.

As Lila's name was spoken, she stepped forward, her hand outstretched. Instead of reaching out her own hand, Victoria Brantford gasped and took a step backward.

After an embarrassed moment, Lila dropped her hand to her side. She could feel her cheeks heating. The other woman had obviously shunned her and she had no idea why.

There was a prolonged moment of silence in the room, broken only by one of the wives' nervous laughter.

"Uh—do you two know each other?" one of the women asked.

Their hostess moved in to dispel the discomfort. "Well, of course they must know each other. Victoria's father is one of the owners of the Chicago team."

As there was no way to deny it, Lila nodded. The question that continued to haunt her was how did Victoria Brantford know *her*, when she was perfectly certain that she had never met the other woman before in her life?

It was Victoria who provided the answer to the question in Cathy Monahan's cornflower eyes.

"Of course I know all about her," the blonde woman said in a high, tight voice. "She's still married to my boyfriend."

One by one, all heads turned toward the woman seated in the corner of the room.

Ignoring the rest, Lila's eyes met Victoria Brantford's gray-green stare. "I've never met you," she said. "How do you know who I am?"

The reply was not the expected one.

"From the pictures," the blonde woman responded, her voice only slightly less taut. "There must be dozens of photographs around his house, all over the place. Your wedding photos. Your high school prom. I've seen them all."

And, apparently, had memorized them all.

Lila was torn between being angry at Cahal for still having the photographs up and daring to show them to his new girlfriend, and being saddened at the thought that he had still lived in that house in Chicago, the one they had picked out together, surrounded by all of their memories.

"After seeing those photographs," Victoria continued, "I could never mistake you."

It was impossible to tell if there was real venom behind that high unnatural voice, so different from the smooth tones that she had used to answer those initial questions from the Wives.

"Maybe I should leave," Lila said, getting to her feet. She gave her hostess an appealing glance. "Surely, there can't be enough room in the club for a girlfriend and an ex-wife."

Ethan's wife was indignant. "I don't see why not! It might never have happened before but there is a first time for everything. It's not as if we were men and incapable of behaving rationally about such things."

This comment earned a few welcomed chuckles.

"I do not see why Lila should leave," Nadia Ivanov added. "She's not just Cahal Wallace's wife, or ex-wife, but she is also going out with Jarrett."

Jack. Lila had almost forgotten him in the turmoil of the past few minutes. Jack had been enthusiastic about her joining the Wives. Perhaps he envisioned them next season posing for the yearly calendar the team put out, the one that included pictures of the players with their families.

There were, somewhere in the distant past of Chicago, pictures of she and Cahal posed for a similar calendar. A younger Cahal and a naïve Lila, smiling into the camera for the benefit of nameless fans.

Without thinking, she turned toward Cahal's girlfriend. "Did he tell you to come here tonight? Did you mention to Cahal that you intended to come?"

Cathy broke in. "I called her, Lila. I asked her to come."

Looking guilty, Victoria waved off her hostess's assistance. "The answer is no on both counts. Cahal never mentioned the Wives and I didn't tell him that I meant to come." She paused before rushing on. "It's just that in Chicago, I could never join. Not when all the women knew you, his wife. I couldn't step into your shadow there. I thought, coming here, I would have the chance of a new start. People would only know me here."

Almost against her better judgment, Lila found herself feeling sorry for the other woman. It was true that she had been an active part of the Chicago club for many years and she had left many friends behind in that city. She could see why Victoria Brantford might have been eager to join the Toronto chapter, to shake off the ghost of her partner's ex-wife. Clearly, she had not expected to actually confront that ghost tonight.

"I should go," Lila again suggested, feeling guilty for being there when the other woman was so obviously disturbed by her presence.

The other women made their protests but she refused to be swayed.

"I'm tired anyways," Lila insisted, "and I promised myself an early night. It was nice meeting you, Victoria."

The blonde woman seemed pleased by this gesture of goodwill. "It was nice meeting you too, Lila. I feel like I know you already."

Lila was taken aback. She hated thinking of Cahal discussing her with another woman, even a rather pleasant one like Miss Brantford. Would he appreciate her speaking about him to Jack? Somehow she thought not.

"Maybe," Victoria went on, "you can show me around Toronto sometime. I've never been here before and I know that you have lived in the city for most of your life."

Lila was forced to admit that that was true and that she did indeed have the time to show a newcomer around the city. Having exchanged phone numbers and said her good-byes, Lila left the Monahans' house, fervently hoping that Victoria Brantford would not take her up on her reluctant offer of hospitality.

Chapter Three

She received the telephone call from her attorney the next day
while she was cataloguing the week's new releases, a task that was
interrupted by the rest of the staff coming over to swipe one of the
books for their own personal consumption before they went on
the shelves. It was one of the perks of the job, of which Lila herself
was apt to take advantage on occasion.

The early hour of the call—it was just past nine—seemed
ominous and Lila prepared herself for the worst. A delay with the
filing of the paperwork perhaps. A lost document that would have
to be re-signed.

The lawyer cut through her vague greetings. "There's a
problem with the divorce motion. Can you come to my office this
afternoon?"

The library was in the north of the city and her lawyer's office
was in the downtown core. She calculated the voyage, weighing it
against the time owing to her from several late nights she'd spent
doing inventory last month.

"I could leave work early." She paused, unsure. "If it's
important."

She could almost hear the lawyer's amused smile. "It is
important." Or else, his tone said, he wouldn't be calling.

Lila confirmed the appointment for three o'clock and hung
up the phone. In a daze for the rest of the day, she allowed all
four copies of the latest novel in her favorite mystery series to
be handed over to her coworkers, leaving none for the shelves,
which meant she would be fending off indignant inquiries about
the book for the next two weeks.

The tall office building housing her lawyer's firm always made
her feel nervous. She had a good lawyer, recommended to her by
one of the wives she'd known in Chicago, originally a Toronto

native, who had been through two messy divorces. Lila hadn't expected hers to be messy, but still wanted the best. The law firm Cahal had retained was housed in the office tower across the street. Adam Billings, her lawyer, came straight to the point. "Your husband wants you to submit to a pregnancy test."

"What?"

This was the last thing Lila expected and she'd spent the entire day coming up with frightening possibilities.

He pushed a sheet of paper across the desk, the top of it stamped "copy" in hard to miss blue ink. He waited while she read over it. When she was finished, Lila looked up with wide angry eyes. "You must be joking."

"I assure you that I am not," Billings replied, "and neither is your husband."

Lila gave him a cool stare. "Well, write that lawyer back and tell him that there is no possibility that I could be pregnant. I haven't seen Cahal in nearly a year, much less gone to bed with him. This is crazy."

"It doesn't have to be your husband whom this request is aimed at," the lawyer advised her. "Frequently, in situations such as these, it is almost certainly not the husband."

She didn't like where the conversation was heading. "What does that mean?"

"I believe that your husband wants to ensure that when a divorce goes through that you are not pregnant with your current boyfriend's child and, shall we say, attempting to pass it off as Mr. Wallace's." There was a hint of admiration in the man's tone. "Your husband's lawyer may be wise to ensure that this test is conducted now. In terms of child support, the legal assumption is that any child conceived during the course of a marriage is presumed to be the child of the two spouses. It would be much more difficult to have a paternity test conducted after a baby was born if the facts were not established now."

Not quite understanding, Lila was silent for a moment. When she spoke again, her words were noticeably subdued.

"Are you saying that my husband thinks I'm trying to pin him down for child support for a non-existent child?"

Adam Billings raised his eyebrows. "Are you saying that there is no chance of pregnancy?"

"I've just told you! I haven't slept with Cahal in a year. I saw him for the first time yesterday. He said—"

She broke off as she remembered exactly what her husband had said.

The lawyer wasn't interested in what Cahal said. "What about your boyfriend?" He glanced down at the pages before him for the name. "Jarrett. Has he recently raised the possibility of having a child? These things have a way of getting out. Could that be why your husband is making the request now?"

Lila shook her head. "Jack and I have only been dating for a short time. I haven't slept with him or Cahal. Or anyone else. There is absolutely no chance that I could be pregnant."

She knew where her lawyer stood in the next sentence. "If there is no pregnancy, there is no harm in taking a pregnancy test," he added. "At a doctor's office, of course. A home pregnancy test simply would not suffice."

The letter was still lying on the desk between them. "What about that? Couldn't you just write back to the lawyer and explain that there is no chance of pregnancy?"

A small smile came to the man's mouth at her suggestion. "I'm afraid that the other lawyer wouldn't take your word for it."

"But we're taking their word that the chance of pregnancy exists," Lila pointed out peevishly. "Well, what will they do if I refuse?"

The answer was prompt. "Your husband will take you to court for an order requiring you to submit to the test and provide the results to his lawyer. Based on the information in this letter, the order would be granted."

"That letter is garbage." She picked it up and began to quote. "'It has come to my client's attention that a possibility exists that Mrs. Wallace may be pregnant. My client wishes to confirm the same.' That's complete nonsense."

The lawyer picked up his own copy of the letter, doing so as if the paper was contaminated by the ugliness of the situation. "It says here that Mr. Wallace was in Toronto two months ago."

"But that's all it says! I never saw him!"

"Now, Lila, there is no need to get worked up..."

The irate expression on her face made him trail off.

"I never saw him," she repeated. "He telephoned my home several times. He might even have come by. I asked my doorman and he remembered someone looking like Cahal but he's not a hockey fan and he couldn't be sure."

"There are specific dates and times mentioned in the letter," the lawyer continued.

"I hope you're playing devil's advocate," Lila said, "and it's not a case where you don't believe what I'm telling you."

Her lawyer looked uncomfortable for the first time since she'd met him. "It's not my tendency to distrust my clients. Of course neither myself nor your husband's lawyer was present during any of these occasions. You must understand my difficulty. If the other party makes this an issue, even if merely to raise the possibility, and we have no evidence to reply, the judge can easily make an order in your husband's favor and you will be obliged to attend a doctor's office to take the pregnancy test."

"I have a reply," she insisted. "I'm denying it. I'll bet you anything that his story will change if he was to testify before a judge, under oath. Then he won't be able to make these vague allegations that we slept together after we were separated."

"If there is a child," Billings remarked, "it would delay the divorce proceedings."

Lila stared at him. "But you said that a divorce would be a mere formality, that no matter how long the financial issues dragged out I could still obtain a divorce after a year of living separate and apart."

"There is one significant exception," the lawyer admitted, "but I didn't mention it at the time because it wasn't relevant."

"What's the exception?"

He was blunt. "A child. No court in this country will grant a divorce if there are no provisions in place for the children of the marriage."

Despite herself, Lila was drawn into the ridiculous discussion of an outcome she knew to be impossible. "How long could it take to make these provisions?"

"As long as it takes to work out the financial issues, often even longer. Custody and access can be highly contested. The system tries to make it easy for couples who have no children to obtain a relatively quick divorce and to deal with the other outstanding issues later. One spouse merely has to prove it is a hardship for them to continue to be married for one reason or another. Usually, one of the spouses wishes to remarry."

"What if someone with a child wants to remarry?"

"Well, the law makes the children the priority. If the parties can agree to deal with the issues of custody and child support and so on beforehand then there is no obstacle to obtaining a divorce. But when the parties are contesting these issues then neither spouse may obtain a divorce until some stability is in place for the children."

Lila admitted that it made sense to put the children ahead of the parents.

"But Cahal could drag those things out forever, just as he's dragging out the financial issues."

The lawyer frowned. "Mr. Wallace does seem to have taken an immovable position on the financial issues."

Lila said, "I don't care if I walk out of the marriage without a penny."

"We've been over this before," Billings pointed out, a hint of impatience creeping into his professional manner. "My advice is straightforward and it is that you are mistaken to give up on your claims for a portion of Mr. Wallace's earnings during your years of marriage. During the years you were his wife, you missed out on opportunities to establish a career of your own due to the demands of his job."

She waved him into silence. They had been over this before and Lila had agreed to keep her options open. If it wasn't for the fact that she'd put her own inheritance from her grandparents' estate into joint accounts, investments and even the house in Chicago, she would have just walked away. She'd already made an offer through her lawyer to take only what she'd received from her grandparents in exchange for ending the financial wrangling, which Cahal had refused. No reason, just stark refusal.

If she contested the pregnancy test then he would drag her into court and that would take precious time. And how would she explain it all to Jack, who expected a deeper commitment—and a sexual relationship—as soon as the divorce came through?

Lila put a hand over her eyes. "I'll take the test as soon as possible. Just tell me where and when."

The lawyer looked relieved. "I will discuss the arrangements with Mr. Wallace's lawyer and my secretary will call you with the necessary information."

*

She seethed all the way home, working herself into a state of high tension. She tried to relax, to think of her dinner with Jack that evening, but she thought instead of Victoria Brantford cuddling up to Cahal while they laughed over her predicament and the blinding anger returned. Her husband was sinking to new depths by the day.

Out of curiosity, Lila read the sports section of the local newspapers that morning, going out of her way to purchase both major publications. Both focused on Cahal Wallace's spectacular victory of the previous night. Both carried photographs. One showed him in his new headshot with his new team, unmasked and smiling into the camera. In it he looked handsome and slightly goofy, grinning in a way people only did for posed official pictures. The other newspaper had a close-up shot from last night's game and it showed a Cahal she'd never known, his face taut and grim, his eyes narrowed as he stared out between the thin metal barriers of his black goaltender's mask. He looked intimidating and almost inhuman.

The man behind the black mask could have done this easily and without a qualm, probably lying between his teeth to his own lawyer and maybe even willing to perjure himself if it came to that. He was determined, she knew that from watching him climb the ranks of the hockey world until he'd emerged on top, and he'd decided to turn some of that power against her.

He'd chosen a sensitive topic. For years, she'd wanted a child and he'd said later when his career was more established. Then when it became clear that he was a success, he'd flatly refused to consider having a family, telling her that he wasn't ready. Knowing his background and the pain caused by his parents' divorce, Lila had tried to be patient. By the time she saw the separation looming, she'd come to recognize his excuses as hollow.

It eased her rage to dream of a future baby for a little while, not the specter Cahal's ludicrous request had raised but a planned and wanted child who would have two stable parents to look after it. After an hour of daydreaming and a long hot bath, she was ready to tell her boyfriend about the last chapter in her divorce saga. She expected him to be angry as she was at the inconvenience but once he understood that Cahal's tactic would not hamper their own relationship she hoped his anger would also pass.

She'd expected anger, she hadn't anticipated Jack's explosive fury. Even in the middle of the dinner rush, with the music and conversation of the restaurant cloaking all but the most strident voices, many of the other diners noticed his fist banging against the tabletop and turned to stare.

"It's no big deal," Lila told him, minimizing her own reaction for his benefit. "I'll just take the test and put the issue to rest."

She watched with some alarm as he finished the contents of his beer mug in one thirsty swallow.

"Then why's he asking for it?"

It took her a minute to understand that this was an accusation and another to realize that she should have had the conversation in private.

Lila reached across the table to touch his hand. "Jack, it's not true. There's absolutely no way I could be pregnant."

He knew that they'd never been lovers so that left Cahal to absolve, something her boyfriend was finding hard to do.

He left her hand where it was, making no move to grasp it. "You said that he tried to contact you a couple months ago. Did you really manage to avoid him as you told me or did he get hold of you somehow? Because I find it hard to believe a persistent guy like Wallace would just give up."

Her smile was crooked. She knew how relentless Cahal could be.

"He didn't just give up, he had to head back to Chicago. I'm sure he would have tried again next time he was in town."

The discussion would have been better suited to his cozy apartment where she could have soothed some of his frown lines with kisses. She was disappointed when the waitress came and Jack ordered another beer.

"What do you think he had to say?"

"Cahal?" she replied with perfect honesty. "I don't know."

After the separation she'd given him no chance to explain anything, afraid he could talk his way out of the worst crimes.

Jack drank his second beer.

"He wants you back."

The suggestion was funny. "Probably," she admitted. "I was the perfect wife and the perfect little fool. Besides, I know how to cook his steaks."

He didn't smile. "He's in love with you, Lila."

"Probably," she said again. "Once upon a time."

The bottom of his mug hit the table with unnecessary violence. "No, not once upon a time. Now."

She sighed. That was the problem with anticipating an argument, she'd been expecting a different one.

"Cahal is not in love with me, Jack. He has a girlfriend." This piece of information caught his attention. "I met her yesterday at Wives. Her name is Victoria Brantford and she came up from Chicago to be with him. Obviously it's not a casual affair."

There was no reason for that fact to hurt as it did, it was both unreasonable and unfair.

Her boyfriend leaned back into the plush upholstery of their booth, again the comfortable and casual man she'd known for the past several months. "What's the girlfriend like?"

She was on easy ground. "Blonde and beautiful. She's much too nice for Cahal, of course."

It was a relief to see him laugh. This time when she reached out, his fingers twined naturally with hers. For the rest of the meal she spoke about work and their plans for taking a vacation together to celebrate her divorce.

"What happens if I get traded?"

The interruption showed he'd been following a very different line of thought while she babbled about their vacation, afraid of a silence that food could not fill.

"Are you being traded?" Lila posed the question with false calm.

"Not that I know of," he said, "but it's not exactly unusual. It's no secret that Clark and Green are trying to put together a championship team and they're willing to spend the money to get the talent they need."

Back-up defensemen didn't come under the heading of talent and for Jack Jarrett's modest salary the powers that be would end up getting another Jack Jarrett. Despite his limited role on the team and occasional appearances on the ice Jack was nonetheless a popular player in Toronto, the kind of gritty scrappy player fans took a liking to for no apparent reason. As far as she could tell, he was the last player in danger of being traded away to another team. It was the 'talented' players who had to always be looking around them, wondering if this was their last game with that particular team.

"You're not going anywhere, Jack. Toronto loves you."

The praise won her a sheepish grin. "I did get a lot of good press about that fight with Amys, didn't I?"

"You pulverized him," Lila, who didn't watch hockey, said. She'd tried watching again after she started seeing Jack but found the tension too difficult to withstand. Even without being on the screen, Cahal's presence was always in the background. Any spectacular save invited a comparison to the premier goaltender in the league and the little segments in between periods, used to update fans on other games that day, often featured him in the highlights. Her husband was not merely talented, he was also quotable and photogenic.

They left the restaurant with their arms wrapped around each other. Across the parking lot, a man shouted Jack's name and he smiled and waved before putting Lila into his car.

"See?" she murmured when he came around to the driver's side. "Everyone in this city loves you."

He flashed her a glance of mingled fondness and mockery. "Everyone?"

Lila straightened. "Jack."

He switched on the ignition. "It's all right," he said. "I'm not pushing."

She found herself wondering why he didn't push. Many men might have and Cahal certainly would. She pushed the thought of her husband firmly away. Jack was not like Cahal, fortunately, and she didn't want him to be any different. A contented man with a solid family background and any amount of loyalty and patience. He was exactly what she needed.

Chapter Four

Adam Billings' secretary called a few days later, but it wasn't to set up the appointment for the pregnancy test. Lila listened to the young woman's conciliatory tone for several minutes, her annoyance rising with each one.

One of the library volunteers entered the staff room and Lila turned her back to the teenaged girl.

"I don't understand why we need this meeting," she said, her irritation no less evident. "I've already agreed to the request."

She couldn't tell how much the young woman knew of the case from her calm professional voice.

"Mr. Billings realizes that this is an inconvenience, Mrs. Wallace..." The woman's voice trailed off, expecting agreement.

Lila did not fail her. There was no point in arguing with the lawyer's underlings, they always retreated behind the mantra of what Mr. Billings wanted, their only goal to ensure that this was attained.

"I can be there," Lila sighed. "Tomorrow at ten o'clock? That's fine."

The summons ensured she spent the rest of the day in a now-familiar fog of uncertainty and worry. After the latest volley from Cahal's camp, she wondered what he could have planned. She knew she wouldn't like the solution.

*

The meeting took place at the office building across the street. The sprawling space housing the law firm might have been cloned from Adam Billings' office. Decorated in muted tones and natural wood, the boardroom oozed expensive understatement.

Cahal and his lawyer were already seated at one end of the enormous table and Lila wondered if they were expected to join them or take seats at the other end, some distance away. Her lawyer appeared to know the protocol, going straight to the occupied side of the room. He shook hands first with the other lawyer, showing wary cordiality, then pumped Cahal's hand.

"Mr. Wallace, I'm glad to meet you. Do you think you can take us all the way to the finals this year?"

Cahal's smile was the polite one often seen in television clips, given to reporters who knew little about sports.

"I intend to give it my best."

Adam Billings' reaction was fatuous. "Good man," he approved. "I've always said that you're just the man Toronto needs between the pipes."

Cahal thanked him and the other man missed the look he sent Lila, a glance that invited her to share his amusement over the lawyer's effusiveness.

"Hello, darling."

Knowing that he was entertaining himself with the intimate look and endearment, Lila nodded stiffly in response.

"Let's get down to the matter at hand." Unlike his client, Cahal's white-haired lawyer was all business. "Mr. Wallace is interested in negotiating a reconciliation. To that end, he is suggesting marriage counseling and renewed cohabitation. He is prepared to cover Mrs. Wallace's legal costs in their entirety in the event that the reconciliation is unsuccessful."

Lila was silent, waiting for her attorney to speak, but for once Billings' glib tongue failed him. His stunned expression irritated her, though it was better than facing her husband's smile.

The other lawyer went on. "Of course you realize, Mr. Billings, that it is our duty as lawyers to present our clients with all reasonable options and opportunities for reconciliation if there is a chance of one."

As her lawyer would not speak, Lila took the lead. "Sir, there is no chance of reconciliation. We're wasting our time having this meeting."

She glared at Cahal, aware that the lawyer would simply carry out his client's instructions. At the prices he was paying, the lawyer would be only too happy to do so. Though Billings' fees were more reasonable—he hadn't been practicing nearly as long as Cahal's attorney—she spent a significant percentage of her salary on legal fees and feared the monthly bills which arrived in her mail with frightening regularity.

"I don't know," her lawyer was saying. "Perhaps you should give the idea some thought. You don't have to make up your mind right now."

Lawyerly caution was not a part of her makeup. Lila stirred in her chair. "I've made up my mind."

The other attorney raised a pair of bushy white eyebrows. "Am I to take it, Billings, that your client is refusing our offer out of hand? Because that's the kind of thing a judge will take into account when it comes to allocating costs."

Costs was one legal term Lila understood; Adam had drilled the concept into her head many times. If one party was unreasonable or merely unsuccessful at any part of the divorce proceedings then they could be compelled to bear not only their own legal costs but also to pay the legal fees for the other side.

Billings spoke to her in an urgent undertone. "We should discuss this in private, Lila."

Her husband's lawyer was helpful. "There are several rooms you may use that are presently vacant."

Cahal's raspy voice cut through his lawyer's. "If we're discussing things in private then it should be Lila and I having the discussion. A reconciliation is a private affair."

Her lawyer's expression was pleading. "Okay," she said, accustomed to taking his advice. After all, it was why she paid him. "I'll give it a try. Adam, come and get me in a half hour."

It was fortunate that she wore a watch, she didn't quite trust her lawyer to stick to the allocated time. He was already punching in numbers on his wireless device, no doubt checking his email.

A secretary posted just outside of the door showed them to a smaller room that was bare of any furniture save for a round table and four chairs. A bottle of imported water and several glasses stood on a tray in the center of the table and she occupied her hands by pouring herself a glass.

Lila leaned her hip against the edge of the table and scrutinized her husband over the rim of the glass.

"What are you up to, Cahal?"

He stood with his back to the door, blocking it as he would a hockey net. There was a glimmer of laughter in those long-lashed gray eyes.

"Darling, you insult me."

"No," she denied, "you insult me by pretending to want a reconciliation eleven months after our separation and one month before we should be divorced. Not to mention the stupidity of that pregnancy test."

"Have you taken it yet?"

"No," Lila admitted. "Instead you sprang this meeting on me. What sort of tactic is this?"

He seemed intent on answering all of her questions with ones of his own. "What makes you think it's a tactic?"

She rolled her eyes to the discreet fluorescent lights overhead. "You make a living anticipating the next move and always being ahead of it."

"This is not a sport." For the moment, he sounded grimly serious.

Lila pulled out a chair and sat down. "Well, if you're not going to come clean then I'm happy to wait here until Adam comes to get me."

"Adam," he repeated the name with a sneer. "On a first name basis with your counsel, are you?"

As this was self-evident, she did not reply but glanced at her wrist.

He came away from the door. "All right, I'll tell you what's going on."

"I knew it was a tactic," Lila murmured, unable to account for the rush of disappointment. "What is the point of this one? Trying to make yourself look good before the judge we're going in front of next month or just continuing in your ongoing attempt to bankrupt me?"

The long stare to which he subjected her made her regret her unthinking words. They'd exchanged financial statements some months ago so he had a fair idea about her financial situation but he didn't know of the mounting legal bills she owed to Adam's firm or the move she'd recently made to a smaller apartment in a slightly seedy part of the city. It was a bachelor apartment, combining living and sleeping quarters into an uncomfortably tiny space, and she was still too ashamed to take Jack there.

"Why haven't you taken any of the support I've offered?"

She adopted his approach and countered with a query. "Is this really how you want to spend your half hour, by going over the same tired ground?"

He shook his head. "No, you're right. Let's discuss this offer. I want a reconciliation because of personal reasons that have nothing to do with you."

The statement stung. "I think it has something to do with me," she responded. "My lawyer explained to me that any reconciliation attempt we made, beyond a certain length of time, may delay my ability to obtain a divorce."

He was frowning. "I hadn't thought of that."

Lila gestured to the chair across from her. "Why don't you explain it? I have to admit that I'm curious."

He sat down and leaned his long arms across the table, fixing her with a piercing stare.

"It's a woman."

She laughed. "Isn't it always?"

The strong talented hands folded into loose fists.

"Her name is Victoria Brantford and her father's a big shot in the States. The family owns a chain of department stores along with a partial share of the Chicago franchise and Victoria's used to getting what she wants."

"And you're what she wants this time?" Lila asked the question.

Cahal grimaced. "She's not my type but I made the mistake of accepting her invitation to some society affair involving the owners of the team and I took her out to dinner a few times afterwards. I thought coming to Toronto that she would get the idea. No luck. She followed me from Chicago."

Lila's throat tightened. She didn't doubt his version of events for a moment. Women always followed him; that was the curse of his looks and talent.

"The daughter of an owner of your team must be hard to shake."

He reached for a clean glass and filled it. "It's even harder when everyone knows you're separated from your wife."

"So you don't want to be separated any longer," Lila concluded. "I get it. You want me to pretend that we've reconciled so you can stop running from this woman. You know, she didn't seem scary."

His head snapped up. "You've met Victoria?"

"Last week." She explained about the meeting at Cathy Monahan's home.

"And Victoria described herself as my girlfriend?"

Lila nodded. "She was very convincing and didn't seem at all dangerous."

"I didn't say she was dangerous," he said. "Only determined."

"That kind of determination can be dangerous."

He stood up with a movement that reminded her vividly of his profession. It amazed her that she could have forgotten. For seven years, she'd unsuccessfully tried to ignore what her husband did at work, trying to pretend that he went to an office instead of a hockey arena, that he rubbed elbows with middle managers instead of admiring reporters and fervent fans.

"I'm not threatened by Victoria, just annoyed." Cahal's eyes touched her but didn't remain. "This is not the first time I've been in this kind of situation. Every athlete goes through the same kind of thing. This time it's different."

He would know; he'd had every kind of stalker over the years, since he was just a young man coming up in the junior leagues. They ranged from crazed super-fans, usually male and middle-aged, to obsessed teenaged girls who treated him like a rock star and who were willing to offer anything for a moment of his time. Alone on the road, some athletes succumbed to the lure of relentless adoration and their spouses were forced to be understanding or seek divorces. Lila had sought revenge.

"How is Victoria different? She seemed quite ordinary to me." Beautiful and far from mentally unsound. The other woman wasn't a teenager to fall for a celebrity who also happened to be close at hand nor did she seem to be a rabid fan of the sport.

Cahal ran his hands through his fair hair, a sign of distress in a man who always followed the team's rules about public appearances and was well-dressed and well-groomed at all times.

"For one thing, Victoria has a background in public relations. She used to plan parties and host charity events for a living. She volunteered for a young senator's campaign last year and was cited as a major influence in his election."

"So she's multi-talented. You should be flattered."

Cahal narrowed his gray eyes. "I am flattered. And if Victoria had left things as they were, perhaps we would be dating by now. She didn't."

Drumming her fingers over the tabletop, Lila asked, "What

was it she did, exactly? Boil your bunny? Write you love letters in her own blood?"

His swift frown told her he didn't find the questions funny.

"I told you, she's not dangerous, just determined." He looked past her. "What she did was launch a publicity campaign. Using pictures of our few public appearances together, she put out a story that we were involved and spread it throughout the Chicago tabloids. Within a month, I was being asked when the wedding was everywhere I went. I tried talking to her. She wouldn't listen. I tried avoiding her. It didn't work. Her father got the owners to give me a lecture about my attitude. They told me that I was starting to act like a superstar instead of playing like one."

"Oh, Cahal."

Lila knew how much that must have hurt when Cahal prided himself on his leadership role on whatever team he played for. His teammates respected and admired him and he never acted like a prima donna. The accusation must have stung and, coming from the owners of his team, there would have been little he could say in return.

She asked, "Is that why you came to Toronto?"

His large frame stiffened. "I didn't ask to be traded, if that's what you're insinuating."

Lila spread her hands out wide. "I wasn't insinuating anything. I know how disruptive disputes between management and players can be and they often end in staffing changes."

"I didn't ask to be traded," he repeated in a voice that was only slightly less disgruntled. "The opportunity presented itself and according to my agent, I would have been a fool to pass up the chance to play in a city more attuned to the hockey culture."

"As well as a city that pays their hockey players quite a bit more money," Lila couldn't resist putting in.

His glance was humorous. "I thought you weren't interested in a financial settlement."

"Ha ha." With a thought to the limited time, she asked, "Where do I come in?"

It was an unnecessary question. Anyone could see where he was leading.

"I need to launch my own publicity campaign," Cahal told her, "with the major story being my sudden reconciliation with my childhood sweetheart."

Lila stared. "It sounds like a fairy tale."

"It will have to," he replied, "to counter some of the stories Victoria's been weaving. This latest incursion on the Wives and Girlfriends here in Toronto is troubling. She tried the same trick in Chicago with terrible results. I didn't think she would attempt the same thing here when she must have known there was a chance of running into you."

The other woman's surprise at their meeting a few days ago appeared genuine but now Lila had doubts.

Cahal went on. "To pull it off, you will have to live with me again and we'll have to spend nearly all of our time together."

"This plan of yours is sounding better and better," she muttered.

"Can you suggest a better one?"

It took her a minute to find the right answer. "It's not my problem."

An ugly smile twisted his handsome face. "It can easily become your problem."

The words were mildly threatening but she was skeptical. "How?"

Bracing his hands against the tabletop, he diminished his height while bringing his face close to hers.

"You gave me the impression that you were anxious to finalize our divorce so you can get engaged to your third-rate defenseman." The unprovoked insult surprised her more than the menacing tone. "Should you fail to help me out, let us say that this divorce could take a much longer time."

Lila looked up. "What have you got up your sleeve?"

His mouth quirked. "Try me."

The price of calling his bluff was more than she could afford to pay.

Lila slumped over the table cradling her face in icy cold hands. "Find someone else, Cahal. A look-alike. An actress. After all this time I can't imagine anyone remembers my face."

"You underestimate yourself."

The comment sounded snide and she shifted a hand to cover one ear. They could clash words all day, they were both very good at it, but at this point simple honesty was her best weapon.

"I can't live under that microscope again."

He leaned across. "Not even on a temporary basis?"

The concealing fingers fell, leaving her uncomfortably bare. "I wouldn't go through that kind of publicity whirlwind for anyone, not even Jack. You're not the man I loved." She paused to let the past tense sink in. "We're not even friends. It's unfair to expect me to do you favors."

"I never stopped being the man you loved."

The intensity of his expression made her wary. They'd gone over this a hundred times and they couldn't agree to save their marriage, what made him think he could convince her now?

She stood. "Time's up. I'm leaving."

The restraining hand he locked around her arm turned into a steadying grip as the door flew open. Her lawyer apologized, his eyes on her husband.

"All ready?" he asked after Cahal glared down the rest of his apologies.

"Yes," said Lila.

"Not quite," said her husband.

Adam Billings looked at his watch. "I'm afraid that's all the time we have, Mr. Wallace. Perhaps another meeting can be—"

Cahal cut in. "I can't waste another day on this. I want it resolved today. Right now."

Lila's lawyer regarded him with a patient stare she knew well. "What exactly is it that we can resolve today? Discussions with your legal counsel have made it clear that we've reached an impasse on the financial issues. At this point the divorce itself is simply a matter of a rubber stamp."

The blonde man smiled; it was the grimace he made behind his mask during particularly grueling matches.

"What about adultery?"

"What of it?" The lawyer knew Lila's accusations and he had counseled her to abandon that ground of divorce, opting instead for the simple basis of having lived separate and apart for the requisite year.

Cahal resumed his leaning pose, completely at ease. "My lawyer tells me that it might delay the divorce if we went down that path, citing adultery as the reason for the separation rather than an unspecified breakdown of the relationship."

Lila held her breath. He wouldn't dare.

Her lawyer made a dismissive motion. "That wouldn't work. Not in this case."

"Why not?"

"Well, first of all you can't rely on your own malfeasance to ground a claim."

Cahal was still smiling. "Meaning?"

The lawyer drew himself up so stiffly that Lila had to hide a grin. "Meaning that your cheating on your wife doesn't allow you to turn around and divorce her."

The smile disappeared although Lila could see that he was expecting that answer. His tall frame was too relaxed for her comfort.

"I don't want to divorce my wife." He shifted his silver eyes to her face. "And I was never unfaithful to her, in body or mind."

Lila rolled her own eyes. She knew just how much faith to put in a pair of gray eyes.

The lawyer shook his head. "Then why bring up the subject?"

"I just thought I'd warn you that I intend to introduce the issue of adultery, which I understand will delay the divorce proceedings significantly." Cahal laughed at the confusion on the other man's face. "Didn't your client tell you? She was unfaithful to me. I have her lover's statement to prove it."

*

Back in the boardroom Cahal's lawyer was as glum as ever. He came prepared with the papers ready for signing, deposited on the tabletop before the two lawyers by another anonymous assistant.

Lila tried to break the silence as the lawyers read from their respective sheets. "Are there really a set of rules for reconciliation?"

Her lawyer frowned at her over the top of the draft contract and she could hear echoes of the lecture he meant to dole out once they were alone.

"There are rules for everything, Mrs. Wallace," the other lawyer intoned.

"Including marriage," her husband added.

"Oh, shut up."

Cahal shook his fair head in mock remonstrance. Unlike his counsel, his smile was very much in evidence. Its sheer intensity was giving her a headache.

His examination complete, her lawyer pronounced the contract equitable and he proceeded to read out highlights to which Lila paid no attention. She was caught and she knew it. Now her only concern was what she would tell Jack. Already her cell phone had twice alerted her to messages he had left while was sitting through the interminable meeting.

"Where do I sign?"

Shaking fingers made her typically neat signature nearly

illegible. Cahal's scrawl accompanied her name on a half dozen copies, followed by the lawyers' tidier script.

Tossing the pen onto the table, Lila asked, "Can I go now?"

Her husband interjected as her lawyer nodded. "Not so fast, darling. We have some things to get straight."

"I can't. Not right now. Jack—"

"Jarrett's not a party to this contract. You are." He flashed false front teeth in another grin. "I'm sure that if you had let him, your counsel would have been happy to explain the consequences of breaking any of the terms."

She ignored her lawyer's grimace. "Jack's as much a part of this as either of us. I'm doing this because of him."

"I'm sure your boyfriend will understand why you have to start living with your husband again. He strikes me as a very understanding guy."

Cahal's exaggerated soothing tones grated as they were obviously meant to do.

"It's none of your business what Jack understands or fails to understand," Lila retorted.

"You're right," her husband told her, his voice suddenly brisk. "If you want your divorce in a few months rather than in a few years, then it makes sense for you to read what you just signed and get used to what's required of you."

Her lawyer repeated the admonishment in more drawn-out terms but the bottom line was the same. In exchange for attempting a reconciliation with her current husband, he would allow her to continue with the divorce proceedings she had launched without challenging the basis for the divorce on the grounds that she was an adulteress. The reconciliation he was proposing was to be for two months, an entire month less than the time set out by the law to nullify the entire separation. According to the country's divorce laws, if they reconciled for more than ninety days, they would have to start the whole process all over again—and wait another year for the divorce to finalize.

"I get it," Lila said. "For the next two months I have to live under Cahal's roof and pretend to be his wife. It doesn't sound so hard. I've had seven years of practice at pretending."

Cahal flashed a grin. "I'd love to help you out with anything you haven't been practicing for the past year."

Lila met his glinting silver-gray eyes. "How do you know I haven't been keeping up with everything we used to do? As we both know, practice makes perfect."

The grin faded to a mere shadow. "And you've proven that you're willing to take extramarital lessons," her husband pointed out.

Adam Billings cleared his throat. "Speaking of which," he said, "I would like to verify the existence of this statement Mr. Wallace alluded to earlier. Is there anywhere I can view it before I leave?"

It hadn't occurred to Lila that Cahal might be lying but that was why she employed a lawyer. His suspicious mind was a match for even Cahal's.

Cahal's lawyer looked at his client and after receiving a slight nod, he produced a legal-sized document from a thin folder. Lila didn't even glance at the copy her lawyer placed before her. She remembered the photographic evidence Chris had shown her—how could she ever forget?

She waited and after a minute a low whistle escaped Adam Billings' lips.

Her lawyer swiveled toward her. "Chris Wallace? That's the other man? Chris Wallace, the number one defenseman in the league, not to mention your husband's cousin?"

"There are other Christopher Wallaces in the world," Lila said.

"But that is the one you slept with," Cahal pointed out without any discernible emotion.

At her lawyer's questioning glance, she lowered her head, acknowledging the identity of the other man. From his viewpoint, as from many others, it would appear as if she had purposely tried to harm her husband by turning to his closest relative in order to wreak revenge for his years of infidelity. The truth was that Chris had been a convenient target, always at hand and immediately sympathetic to her plight.

Lila turned to her lawyer. "Do I have to listen to this? It can't be in the contract."

Billings swept his papers together. "You're right, it isn't. Lawyers are no longer required for what you and your husband have planned for the next two months. Once the time is over, you can contact me and we will begin completing the final steps for the divorce."

The words were more final than she expected and with a startled look at the other men, she followed Billings out of the door and down the hallway. Even knowing that she would be billed for any further conversation, she was not willing to part with him yet.

"What do I do now?"

As they reached the lobby of the massive building, he slanted her a glance that encompassed some of his former good humor.

"That depends on you, Mrs. Wallace. As I told you upstairs, the lawyers' roles are over for the time being. What you need now may be a therapist or marriage counselor."

Lila brushed this suggestion aside. "I don't need a marriage counselor for a pretend reconciliation."

Her lawyer glanced around at the surging flow of people before drawing her into a less trafficked corner of the lobby. "I would advise you not to speak of the real nature of your marriage reconciliation in public. One of the terms of the contract you just signed restricts you to secrecy."

"What about Jack? I assume that he's an exception."

Adam Billings shook his head. "There are no exceptions save for your respective legal counsel and we are bound by solicitor-client privilege. I couldn't breathe a word about this case even if I wanted to, or else I would lose my license to practice law."

She caught his suited arm. "We have to go back upstairs. You have to negotiate an exception for my boyfriend. I have to be able to tell him about this contract or he'll believe..."

Her words trailed off as the full effect of what she had agreed to infiltrated.

"Or he will believe what everyone else will believe," her lawyer concluded. "That you and your husband have reconciled in order to give your marriage another shot."

He was staring at her and she remembered that even he didn't know the true motive behind the fiction of the reconciliation. No one knew that save for she and Cahal.

Chapter Five

With enough money, any chore could be made easy, even a pretend reconciliation. Lila's possessions moved without the need for her to lift a hand in aid. Her clothes, her books, even her knickknacks and cosmetics flew across the city, shuttled by hired professionals, and all she had to do was follow in their path. As disconcerting as it was to find her clothes arranged on hangers and in drawers, her perfume bottles ranged along a glass-topped dressing table, almost as if she had done it all in her sleep, it was also a relief. Her possessions fit in well, now it was her turn.

"It's a nice place," she commented, the words inadequate to describe the lake-facing penthouse suite with its floor-to-ceiling windows along one long wall and stark contemporary furniture. It was far from the comfortable traditional house in Chicago and she guessed that that was the point of the stringent modernity.

"It's your home now," Cahal replied, his tone one she didn't like to analyze.

Lila couldn't resist adding, "Only for the next two months."

"We'll see."

Clenching her fists, she said nothing.

It had all happened so quickly. One day she was looking forward to a new life and the next she was back in time, back in a marriage with a man who had always made her feel jealous and insecure. No, not always. When they were teenagers and Cahal's star was just rising, she'd been proud of him and never suspicious. His successes felt like hers and she knew he felt the same about her education and career. What happened? Was it just the fame seeping between them, eventually forcing them apart, or was it more?

A peal of classical music caused her to search out the purse she'd dropped on Cahal's leather couch, scrambling her cell phone from its depths. She'd turned it on only minutes ago, aware she couldn't hide indefinitely.

"Lila?" Jack's familiar voice held an odd mixture of relief and anger. "Where have you been for the past two days?"

First at her lawyer's office and now back under her husband's roof? Those words weren't easy to say, on top of being perfectly ludicrous.

She settled on, "It's a long story." *Even longer beneath Cahal's mocking eyes.* Lila turned her back on him. "Can we meet somewhere and talk?"

"I've got practice tonight." He sounded aggrieved.

"How about afterwards?" Her dark eyes were on Cahal, aware that he could hear every word of their conversation due to the other man's raised voice. She added, "We've really got to talk."

Jack's laugh was hollow. "That doesn't sound good."

She swallowed. "It's not."

A short pause followed before he said, "Tell me now."

"I can't," she said. Not if she wanted to be free to be with him.

"Where are you?" Jack demanded. "I'll skip practice and come get you."

"No, no, don't do that," she protested. "It's just the kind of thing that'll put you in Coach's black books."

"I don't care," he insisted. "I'm worried about you. *My* career doesn't come before you."

The clear emphasis made Cahal turn and walk over to the glass wall. As dark as it was now early in the evening, little could be seen of the lake outside except for the shimmering smooth surface beneath pale moonlight and the occasional fleeting path of a boat.

"I'll meet you at the arena after practice," she said into the phone. "I'll tell you...what I can."

"Lila," he hesitated for a fraction of a second, "I love you."

Though she closed her eyes, silent tears slipped out. "I know."

Cahal didn't turn. "You can't tell him anything about our reconciliation without violating our contract."

Flipping the tiny silver phone shut, Lila brushed away the tears with the back of her hand. "I know that, too."

His broad back was rigid. "So what are you going to say?"

She tossed the cell phone back into her purse and flopped down on the couch next to it. "I don't know. Why don't you tell me? You're probably dying to."

He came away from the windows, his movements powerful yet supple, breathtaking in such a large man. He sat a careful distance from her, his denim-covered thighs spread and his strong hands dangling between them. His hands were beautiful, swift and expert, and the remembered touch of them made her shiver. This was the last thing she wanted, to rekindle a fire from the ashes.

Silver eyes traced her features. "I'm not trying to hurt you, Lila."

She laughed unsteadily. "Since when do you have to try?"

He ought to know better; his life was governed by impulse and instinct. The worst infractions were often committed without any intention to injure but the results were still catastrophic.

"This is for the best, Lila."

"Dammit!" She leaped to her feet. "You think you know it all, don't you?"

He rose, too, but she'd never been intimidated by his size.

"No, I don't think I know it all. I just happen to know you."

"I've changed," she insisted.

"You still love me," he said. His voice was supremely confident, as if he was stating a naked truth.

"Loved," she corrected. "Past tense."

His mouth curved but not in a smile. "You never stop loving that first one."

First what? First love or first lover? Perhaps she had been his first love but she doubted that she was his first lover. Certainly she wasn't the last.

"Love," she repeated the word with a bitterness that surprised even her. "It's readily offered as a solution when so often it's the source of the problem."

Cahal thrust his hands in his pockets. "Are you telling me you don't believe in love?"

Lila frowned. "I believe in trust and security."

"And love comes after these?"

She wasn't certain about that but she knew what she had to say to shut him up.

"For me, yes."

He freed his hands then he pushed them through his flaxen hair. "I can give you those things, Lila. If you still believe I cheated—"

"I don't believe it," she cut in. "I know it."

She had proof. Evidence. Details.

"And your source is unimpeachable?"

She looked him straight in the eye. "Cahal, I've told you before. I know you entertained women in your hotel suite while you were on the road. I know it. When you deny the truth, it just makes it worse."

"What truth do you know of?" His voice was contemptuous. "I've never had a woman in my hotel room. Ever. It's against the team rules and it's against my moral values."

His moral values! She couldn't hold back a snort. Yet he was so adamant. So very believable.

Stubbornly, she'd wanted him to admit the truth before she showed him her proof but he never could. She realized that now.

Pulling out her phone, she said, "I know you had a blond woman in your hotel room in Los Angeles. She came around eleven and she left after midnight. Here is the proof you wanted."

Turning her screen toward him, she displayed the first photograph of the woman's back entering the hotel room, the room number displayed prominently on the opening door, with no more than a sliver of her husband's face beyond. The time stamp on the photograph showed that it was 10:56 p.m. Silently, she turned to the next photograph. 12:38 a.m. The room number was the same. Cahal's face was plain in the opened doorway as he showed the woman off, his head bent down toward hers as if they had just kissed.

He took a deep breath and blew it out in frustration. "Anyone is capable of lies if they have the right motivation."

He wasn't denying it!

"There's an innocent explanation, Lila. That woman—Carrie Jones—works for my agent."

"Convenient," she said.

His motives were all too transparent. Good publicity made their marriage necessary to his public image and a last-minute reconciliation before their divorce—a true one—would provide priceless press. On a personal level, he had kept her the perfect docile wife for a long while and perhaps he thought that state was again obtainable.

"Do you honestly think Victoria is the first woman to chase after me?" he asked. "Even knowing that I was married doesn't stop some people. But this woman was there for truly innocent reasons."

That word again! Innocent. There was nothing innocent about him. He lied until he was found out, then he lied some more.

"It's a problem," he said. "But I only point it out to show you that anyone who tells you that I was unfaithful might have another motive—to ruin our marriage. Have you even questioned why someone was watching and taking pictures of my hotel room?"

"Because they couldn't have you?" she asked sweetly. She knew that one of his teammates had taken the pictures as a joke, then sent it to Chris, who sent it on to her. As far as she knew, the whole league knew about her husband's infidelity before she did.

A corner of his mouth jerked upwards. "You must find that unbelievable. When did you stop wanting me? Before or after that expensive university education?"

Close to a violent reaction, Lila spun around so that his contemptuous face no longer filled her vision. "Go to hell, Cahal. Just go to hell and leave me alone."

"No chance," his raspy voice shot over her shoulder. "If I'm going to hell, I'll make sure you're there to keep me company."

At the moment she had no choice except to believe him. He'd shown that he wasn't a man to make idle threats.

"Your idea of marriage is more like indentured servitude," Lila muttered.

He smiled. "And I was going to offer you a ride down to the arena to meet your boy toy. How many slave masters would be so considerate?"

"He's not my boy toy," she delayed. How would it look to Jack if she showed up with her husband? "Jack is my boyfriend."

"We could argue your right to have a boyfriend while you and I are still lawfully married. A lot can occur in two months."

"Miracles are rare," Lila replied, coming to a decision. Between the cold and Cahal, Cahal won by a slim margin. "We'd better get going or you'll be late for practice."

"Oh no!" His features formed into an expression of mock terror. "I wouldn't want to end up in Coach's black books."

"Oh, shut up."

Before she could reconsider the cold bus ride, Cahal swept up his car keys and jangled them noisily. "Coming?"

Music from a satellite radio station filled the void of silence during the short trip. As short as the ride was, it was enough time for Lila to build up a dread of seeing her boyfriend again. Without a proper explanation, the reasons for her apparent reconciliation with her husband were baffling.

The arena parking lot held few cars, allowing Cahal to ease his sports car into a space close to the entrance. This time there was no crush of reporters eager for gossip. No one from the local media was even aware of the fact that the biggest bombshell in sports celebrity news had already quietly taken place on the preceding day. She mused that perhaps after this the local sports pages would start posting reporters outside of the offices of prominent city divorce lawyers, awaiting the next hot scoop.

Lila stood by the entrance while Cahal retrieved his equipment from the trunk. The heavy bag was so much a part of his identity that she ceased to see it. In her experience, all men were hockey players and all men were untrustworthy. Except for Jack.

Jack.

"Are you okay?"

Her husband's low question forced her to glance up to meet his eyes, shaded a dark pewter with concern. Artificial concern, Lila amended. If he cared about her, he wouldn't have manipulated them into their present position.

"I'm fine," she answered.

"You look pale," he observed. "Are you sure this is the best time for this? You've just moved, uprooting yourself from the life you've known for the past twelve months. You can talk to Jarrett tomorrow or next week."

Ignoring his perfectly reasonable suggestion, Lila pointed out, "By then the news of our reconciliation will be in all the papers in the city. I can't let him face that without at least a warning."

Her husband shrugged one broad shoulder. "Suit yourself."

His tall figure disappeared into the bowels of the arena while she found her way to the bleachers where the only other occupants of the building were gathered. The group consisted of coaches and assistants, all of whom looked up curiously as she approached. One face lit up with recognition.

"Lila Wallace! What are you doing here?"

Lila smiled at the squat man, a former assistant coach from the

Chicago bench. "I live in Toronto," she replied, submitting to an awkward hug. "I could ask you the same thing, Harry."

"I got a job up here," Harry Cole told her. "Following your hubby. Or should I say..."

Noting the older man's sudden embarrassment, she figured it was as good a time as any to begin spreading the pre-approved story.

"It's all right, Harry. Cahal and I are back together."

The man's smile was both relieved and knowing. "I suspected something of the kind was in the works when your husband began agitating for that trade. As far as I knew the only connection he had up here was you."

For a moment she stared. "Both of Cahal's parents live a few hours out of the city," she finally managed to say.

The other man grinned. "And I'm sure he moved to Toronto to be close to his folks. Well, I'm glad it worked out, Lila. You've got a good man there and he deserves to be happy."

What about what she deserved? Did she deserve to be alone and miserable, to be lied to and cheated on for years? She said nothing as Harry drew away, called to the ice by a shout.

The players were just getting warmed up, sprawled out on the ice stretching or skating in lazy circles. Usually one of the first to hit the ice, Jack hadn't arrived yet but Cahal's tall figure was soon conspicuous, clad in the thick protective layers essential to goaltenders.

"I knew you would have to show up eventually."

Lila's head turned to meet the owner of the frosty voice and was surprised to find that it belonged to Cathy Monahan.

"Hello, Cathy. What are you doing here? I thought you hated watching practice."

The blonde woman grimaced as she plunked down in the seat beside Lila. "It's not my first choice for entertainment but I've been forced to come for the past few weeks, hoping to corner some of my absentee members."

Lila flushed as she recalled having skipped the last meeting of the Wives and Girlfriends.

"We need your help for the Christmas party," Cathy went on, referring to the annual charitable event where fans paid dearly for the opportunity to dine with their favorite players and bid on hockey merchandise. "There's only a month left and positions are going swiftly but you're lucky since I saved you a good one. I heard what a great job you did in Chicago."

The promise of a good position in the party committee sounded ominous. After only a handful of meetings, Lila knew that the other women avoided being assigned tasks by Cathy, who was noted for being difficult to please.

"I built up connections in Chicago," Lila was forced to point out, "doing publicity and so on. It's not the same in Toronto. You would be a far better position to do what has to be done."

The other woman laughed as she straightened in her seat. "I don't intend to offer you my job, dear. I've been organizing the Christmas party for the past three years."

Lila turned again to watch the skaters. "Then why do you need me?"

Cathy Monahan altered her tone. "Your ideas are terrific. I heard that Chicago broke all the records for annual contributions when you organized that player bachelor auction."

"It was good publicity," Lila agreed, a reminiscent smile breaking across her face. "One of the players, Greg Anderson, ended up married to the woman who placed the highest bid for him. She was a surgeon at the local hospital."

"That's exactly the kind of buzz we need to generate," the blonde woman enthused. "Maybe not a bachelor auction since there aren't too many bachelors left on our team but perhaps another kind of auction. Win a day of hockey with your favorite player or dinner with your favorite star."

Lila didn't point out that such prizes were not altogether

uncommon, which was why she had chosen the unique prize of a date with a bachelor player. A group of eager female bidders was a sight to see, with some younger members of the crowd waving stacks of their parents' money for the chance at private time with their dream date.

"What about a pin-up calendar with the players in racy poses? It works for the firefighters. Or merchandise featuring the players at home with their families. That would be perfect for Christmas and some of the wives are very photogenic. You and Nadia, for a start."

Cathy pulled out a small notebook and began making rapid notes. "Those are great ideas, Lila, but don't forget yourself. I'll bet you take good pictures and Jack would be thrilled to pose next to you. Make it official and all that."

The other woman's words forced Lila to swallow hard as the figures on the ice surface blurred. Thankfully, Cathy didn't notice.

"Now, about that job I've got planned for you."

The blonde woman prattled on but Lila was no longer listening.

Jack Jarrett had just taken the ice and his path took him straight to Cahal's net. It was too far to tell what the men were saying. Other skaters came to a halt as Jack's voice lifted above the general din and even Cathy Monahan stopped talking.

"Isn't that your hus...uh...boyfriend?"

Lila was already skipping over the rows of benches as she scrambled down to the ice. Leaning over the boards, she had to push her head between the elbows of a pair of players who were resting and watching the situation unfold. The two men across the ice were facing off, Jack's face bright red beneath his helmet and Cahal's paler than normal. Even from a distance it was obvious that the defenseman was the aggressor, coming nose to nose with the taller man several times yet the goaltender backed off each time, sliding back to put a few inches between the two.

"Can Wallace fight?" One of the nearby players asked beneath his breath. "From the way he's backing down, it doesn't look like it."

"Oh, he can fight," his companion stated. "I was on the ice when he nearly took Trevor Collins' head off. It was the final game of the series and Collins kept crowding the crease."

"I still put my money on Jarrett."

"I'll take that bet."

Gloved hands met inches from Lila's face, sealing the wager. She wanted to yell at them to stop behaving like fools and intervene, but the players would be the first to tell her that such diplomacy wasn't a part of their job description and in fact could hurt their reputations. The only action worse than backing down from a fight was forcing another man to back down from one.

Jerking her attention to the far ice, Lila saw the two men circling each other. Neither pair of hands were raised, yet there was anticipation in every lazy step and in the collectively held breath of all watching.

"Hey! Hey, what's going on here?" The assistant coach's quick stride brought him to a stop between the two men. "Wallace, you're supposed to be practicing poke checks. Jarrett, you're not playing tomorrow so you can get undressed and head home."

Jack's mouth fell open. "Wh—"

"You heard me." The smaller man's voice rang out strong if a little unsteadily. "Hit the road, Jarrett. I'll see you tomorrow."

For a moment it looked like the defensemen would resist, his belligerent stance stiffening rather than relaxing, then he gave a shake of his head and turned away, skating off ice and lumbering toward the dressing rooms. His exit occurred in silence.

The assistant coach's orders rang out again. "All right, Parker, you're with me. Let's see some speed. Ivanov, you team up with Efflin. Look alive, boys."

Cahal skated back to his net, his color restored. He didn't look toward Lila but she knew he had to be aware of her presence, otherwise he wouldn't have backed away from Jack's challenge.

Cathy Monahan appeared at her elbow. "What was that all about?"

"Beats me."

"Yeah, right."

"Look," Lila said carefully, "I don't want to discuss it, all right?"

The other woman was silent, no doubt debating the merits of probing any further but she must have sensed Lila's willingness to walk away, for she kept quiet on the subject of the aborted fight, reverting back to the topic of the party.

Not paying any attention, Lila was wondering if she ought to keep her date with Jack or wait for her husband. After the incident on the ice, it would be a choice of which of the two men was less angry and embarrassed.

Cahal took the decision away from her by skating up to the two women at the first break in his exercises. He greeted the blonde woman with an impersonal smile after which he directed all of his comments to his wife.

"Don't go anywhere with Jarrett tonight."

It was pointless to ask why.

"What were the two of you saying out there?" Lila posed the question, aware that Cahal could have chosen any of those tense minutes to inform Jack of their newly reformed marital arrangement and destroy all her chances for the future.

"Nothing that you should be saying," was his surprising answer. "I didn't tell him about us, Lila. I know you wanted to do that."

"I did," she stammered, lifting disbelieving eyes to his set face. "I do!"

He flicked her cheek with an icy glove tip. "I've heard that before," he said before skating back to the net.

Cathy Monahan looked dazzled. "Wow, is that your husband? I've never see him up close. He's gorgeous!"

"He's okay," Lila said.

"Okay?" The other woman slid her a sidelong glance. "What *is* going on between the two of you?"

On the verge of giving a sharp reply, Lila belatedly remembered the role she was supposed to be playing. Lowering her eyelids, she murmured, "It's complicated."

Cathy frowned suddenly. "What about Jack and Victoria?"

This time Lila didn't have to pretend confusion. "It's difficult when other people's feelings are involved."

"I should say! Victoria deserves to know what Cahal's intentions are," the other woman claimed. "After all he did drag her here from Chicago. She thinks they're going to get married."

"She should think harder," Lila said. "I mean, our divorce isn't final as of yet."

Cathy planted her hands against the top of the encircling boards, the back of her hands nearly white from the pressure. "Yet you became involved with Jack Jarrett."

Biting back an angry reply, Lila stared out over the ice at the blurred figures. Her stomach was churning and her conscience wasn't faring any better.

Cahal's silly ruse was having unexpected results, none of them welcome.

Chapter Six

The practice ended early on a depressed note. Cahal drove them home after first walking her conspicuously to his car, the fortuitous parking spot finding another use. By the end of the day, the entire team and their extended families would know that something was happening between the divorcing couple. But would Jack?

Back at the penthouse, she retreated to her bedroom to try Jack's cell phone number several times, all unsuccessful. Wherever he was, he didn't want to be reached.

Just before ten, Cahal poked his head in the door. "Dinner."

Lila looked up from her perch atop a thickly padded trunk, one of the pieces of furniture Cahal had salvaged from their house.

"I'm not hungry."

Pushing the door wider, he stepped into the room. "You must be, you haven't eaten."

Turning her face away, she insisted, "I'm not hungry and it's too late anyway. Go ahead without me."

"Too late?" Cahal's deep voice lost some of its wary patience. "We always ate dinner at this time."

"We did," she agreed, "because this was the time you came home from evening practice and I had to be accommodating. To me, it always felt as though we were eating in the middle of the night. We used to go to bed right after."

He moved forward on strong limbs, coming to crouch beside her makeshift window seat. "To bed," he reminded her, "but not to sleep."

His proximity forced her to turn her head; it was difficult to ignore him at a distance and impossible at close range. Smoke-gray eyes regarded her yet the look in them was far from calculating. That look transfixed her.

"Lila." His raspy voice lowered to a mere abrasion of sound, caressing, inviting.

With a smothered groan, he pushed his fingers through the dark curtain of her hair, his hand cupping the curve of her skull to bring her closer. She didn't resist the inexorable pressure nor did she comply, simply letting it gather her in its tide.

Slowly his mouth lowered to hers, exerting the same inescapable force, undemanding yet irresistible.

The kiss was as tentative as a teenager's, as sweet as their very first. She was trembling. This was Cahal, her first, her only. Still her only.

Until she tasted the tang of salt on her lips she wasn't aware of crying. Tasting her tears, Cahal drew back, his expression altering.

"Baby—"

She pushed against his arm, not hard but enough to move him, and he went without protest, his mouth hard.

"Not now, Cahal."

His tone matched the set of his mouth. "When?"

Lila forced her limbs to untangle and move away from the trunk, away from him. "I don't know. Perhaps never. This... situation is not exactly conducive to romance."

He stood up. "I'm not talking about romance. I'm talking about a relationship. Our relationship."

Meeting his eyes unblinkingly, she told him, "Our relationship is over. This charade merely put it on life support."

"There's nothing wrong with a little professional intervention. I suggested it at the time."

It took her a minute to figure out what he meant and then the reminder was irritating.

"We went over this a dozen times," she said, pushing past him. It was unnerving to have this conversation in her bedroom; it already felt stamped with his presence. "No amount of marriage counseling could have explained away your cheating."

He followed her across the living area. "I never cheated on you."

The anger below the surface of his claim was just barely contained.

"And I will never believe you," Lila said, sitting down to the dinner he had laid out.

"Because of Chris?"

Her dark head jerked up from her contemplation of the cooling food. "What do you mean?"

During their worst arguments, she never disclosed the source of her information and she was still somewhat surprised that he had never guessed. Chris Wallace was the one who had given her the proof of Cahal's affair, passing along the photographic evidence he'd received from another player. Of course, Chris must already have suspected something was up. He had had ample opportunity to observe his cousin on the road, for the two played together on a series of junior teams, both local and international. Although in constant competition during their adult years, the two men also held a healthy respect for one another. She felt that she could trust Chris better than his cousin, particularly when his cousin had a good reason to lie—to save his marriage. Chris had never married.

Though he held his knife and fork ready, Cahal made no attempt to begin eating. "Have you considered that counseling might have helped me deal with your affair?"

Lila frowned. "I thought the team forced divorcing players to see a therapist."

"Alone, yes. But they couldn't force you to participate."

The cool tone reassured her. He couldn't know that Chris had been the one to tell her about her husband's infidelities. Enough tension existed within the extended Wallace family to add this additional stress.

"What did you do?" The question nearly choked her. For nearly a year, she had tried to forget Cahal Wallace and every situation that might have reminded her of him. Now that she could assuage her curiosity, she was realizing that the answers would be refined torture. "How did you deal with our break-up?"

A pained smile curved his mouth as he set down his utensils. "Surprisingly, it was my aunt and uncle who came to my rescue. They were appalled by their son's behavior—they came down so hard on Chris that I felt guilty about adding my own blame— that they tried to make up for it themselves. They called every Sunday, flew over whenever they could make it, invited me over for holidays."

"What did Chris do for the holidays?"

Her question was automatic; the image of his cousin spending lonely winter days by himself, without even the challenge of his job to distract him, saddened her.

Cahal got up and walked over to the liquor cabinet, filling a glass with clear liquid and downing half of its contents before he sat down again.

"Chris was never interested in family," he said. "He was never interested in anything except playing hockey...and you."

"Me?"

He lifted the glass in a mocking gesture. "It's to your credit that you never realized it and his that he never pushed it to your attention. But he was always patient."

Eyeing the now-empty glass skeptically, Lila couldn't quite take in what he was saying. If Chris was behind an elaborate scheme to break up his cousin's marriage, he didn't ultimately benefit from it. She was dating Jack, not Chris Wallace.

"I don't think Chris would—"

Cahal broke in. "I don't care to hear what my cousin is or isn't capable of doing."

His savage expression silenced her for several minutes as they both attempted to eat the congealed food on their plates. After a short time, Lila gave up but her husband demolished the cold chicken and vegetables, his metabolism too quick to allow him to skip a meal. Even so, Lila saw that the features she had once loved were leaner than ever, the planes of cheek and jaw pronounced.

Trying to put the conversation on neutral ground, she inquired after his parents.

"Dad's doing great," Cahal replied with a real smile this time. "My little brothers and sister are growing up quickly." The smile faded. "My mother is in the middle of another stint in rehab."

This last piece of news was momentous. In more than a dozen years of begging, threatening and cajoling, Dina Wallace had only agreed to attend rehab once before, just prior to her son's wedding. She fell off the wagon the following year.

"Wish her luck for me."

"I'd prefer not to mention your name to her," he told her. "The news of the separation hit my mother hard. She always believed in our perfect fairy tale marriage."

"Fairy tale," Lila repeated. "I suppose that makes you the prince and me...Cinderella?"

"Don't start down this road again." His tone was sharp and hard. "We're from the same place, you and me."

Lila's upper lip curled. "Lower middle class urban fringe dwellers."

Cahal pushed his empty plate aside. "I thought Chris was the only one with that particular chip on his shoulder."

"And I thought we weren't talking about your cousin."

He clamped his mouth shut. "Fine. Let's talk about something else."

Picking up her plate, Lila decided, "I'm finished talking. I'm going to bed."

He joined her at the sink with his dishes. As always, he picked up a sponge and lent a hand instead of letting her do the chores alone. It was a habit left over from the days when their time alone was precious and too short and every minute together was spent together.

After a minute, he spoke. "I don't want to fight."

She looked up from drying her hands. "Why? Are you going on the road tomorrow?"

"Yes." His answer was terse.

"Surprise, surprise." It was always his way to leave the house with a smile and a kiss, never with a grievance simmering between them. Well, she wasn't his wife anymore, not in any real sense, and she had no intention of towing the line any further than she was contractually obligated.

"Goodnight, Cahal."

*

An hour later, she was still wide awake. It was more than the strange bedroom, which, although filled with her familiar things, was too big and chilly. At that altitude, the wind blew stronger, whistling against the windows from across the lake.

Old habits were difficult to break and the rule against going to bed angry was more than a habit, it made good common sense.

Wrapping a fluffy robe around her skimpy nightgown, Lila braved the cold floor down the hall to Cahal's bedroom. A tap on the door failed to rouse him so she knocked louder and louder, unable to believe he was asleep so early.

"Looking for me?"

The raspy voice at her back made her jump and she swiveled around with her hand at her heart.

"You scared me!"

"Sorry." The apology was perfunctory. Reaching around her, he opened the door to his bedroom. "Did you want something?"

He hadn't bothered with a robe and the flannel pajama bottoms he wore against the winter night left his chest bare. Once smooth and tanned, the broad muscles were now covered by crisp golden hair.

He stared down at her. "What is it, Lila? I have to be on a plane first thing tomorrow."

The razor sharp edge of impatience in his voice shackled her tongue.

Swallowing, she recovered her voice. "Don't be angry," she pleaded. "We can't go to bed angry."

His gray eyes were shining for just a moment before he hardened them into stone pebbles. "It was my parents' rule to never go to sleep angry. See how well it worked for them."

With an inarticulate murmur, she touched his arm, instinctively seeking to comfort. The toned skin, covered by gold hair, was like living steel beneath her fingers, warm and exciting.

"Divorce must be a disease," he muttered. "Everyone in this family catches it."

Lila protested. "What about your aunt and uncle? They're happy together."

"They're going through a trial separation," Cahal informed her. "Happy times all right."

The news hit her hard. "A separation? Joe and Sheila?" Her thoughts went to their son. "Poor Chris."

It was the equivalent of pouring lighter fluid onto a dying fire. Cahal's entire body tensed.

"You've always had a soft spot for him," her husband accused, the words as soft as a whisper. "What is it about him that attracts women?"

As hurtful as it was to be lumped into an impersonal category along with Chris' numerous girlfriends, Lila tried to answer.

"He possesses the advantages you have, Cahal. He's attractive and successful. He's generous and considerate. He's fun to be around."

"He's good in bed," Cahal put in *sotto voce*.

How awful to admit she didn't remember. "I don't want to discuss that," she told him.

"And I don't want to be compared to your lover," he countered, "but here we are in the middle of the night doing just that."

"Cahal..."

A movement dislodged her hand from his arm and he brushed by with a grin and a waft of soap. "You've apologized and I've forgiven you."

She sputtered, "*You've* forgiven *me?*"

He turned to lean on the doorframe, the grin still very much in evidence. "Big of me, isn't it?"

"Bastard."

His expression became abruptly solemn. "Such language. I thought you liked my parents."

"What's that got to—" Lila trailed off as a big arm hooked her waist and lifted her into the bedroom. Quick as the motion was, she was left breathless but unbruised. Cahal's controlled strength always amazed her.

The spacious room she had been hauled into was large, dominated by the custom-made bed they had shared in Chicago, but nonetheless smaller than her room down the hall. Decorated in neutral tones complemented by natural wood, it was effortlessly elegant and expensive; a masculine room that didn't exclude feminine tastes.

"This is your bedroom," she protested, sounding like an affronted virgin.

"Yes." He nodded gravely. "It's where I sleep and also where I finish arguments."

No woman would be capable of arguing beneath that splendid golden body.

A stab of jealousy made her sharp. "We're not arguing," she insisted. "We're making up. I want to go to sleep."

The arm still locked around her hips tightened. "Me too, baby. In this big bed, but not alone."

Lila struggled against the restraining grip. "Well, don't expect me to join you."

His mouth touched the top of her head. "Why not? This is the usual place for making up."

By bracing her hands against his chest she was able to put a few inches of space between them. Conscious of the warm bare skin beneath her palms, Lila felt her blood pound through her body.

"When we were married, yes," she conceded. "Not now."

He narrowed his gray eyes to silver slits. "We're still married."

Her mouth curved. "And we're both obligated to follow out the terms of the contract. This is not part of it."

Cahal's hands slid down to the small of her back, pressing them together from chest to hip. The feel of his hard body was refined punishment. Unconsciously her fingers spread invitingly over his chest muscles and she felt them contract beneath her hands.

His fair head lowered. "No," he murmured, "this is a bonus."

Lila met his mouth readily, the flame he had kindled earlier fanned to life.

No longer tentative, his lips were nonetheless exploratory, re-learning the shape and taste of her mouth at his leisure. But Lila didn't want to go slow. Too many thoughts intruded and she wanted to squash them.

Tilting her head, she forced the kiss to deepen to an open-mouthed exploration.

He groaned her name as his mouth left hers to sear the side of her neck with furious kisses, pushing past the thin barrier of her robe to scorch the silken curve of her shoulder. He gripped her so tight that his fingers bit into her skin yet she barely noticed as she clutched his biceps, reveling in the rock hard strength.

Too long she'd slept in a lonely bed, remembering how good it had been with this man, remembering the first shy encounters in the back seat of his car, the night of his proposal when they consummated their relationship for the first time, the hours after he came back from a particularly grueling stint on the road. Always she greeted him with warmth and love and all of those times he'd been cheating on her.

Breaking off the kiss, Lila gasped for breath, hardly aware of the soothing motions his fingers made over her bare arms. Her robe was in a puddle by her feet.

He nuzzled her neck and throat. "Too quick?" He groaned as his lips clamped down on her exposed skin. "It's been so long."

Lila ignored the blood singing in her ears. She loved him but she had been down this road before.

Making her voice cold, she told him, "For you, perhaps. Not for me."

Stepping out of the warmth of his arms, she let him draw his own conclusions about her meaning. He knew about his cousin, of course, but his likely assumption about Jack would be wrong—she had never slept with her boyfriend.

"You want this, Lila." The raspy words were persuasive. "Don't deny it."

"I won't. I just don't forget my promises that easily."

His upper lip curled in a fierce scowl. "To Jarrett, you mean? You made a promise to me that predates anything you and he had going."

It terrified her how easily he could dismiss her relationship, placing it firmly in her past. If he knew the truth...

Her barriers already paper-thin and scorched by his nearness, Lila squeezed her eyes shut to block out the strong temptation of his muscled chest.

"I can't go through this again, Cahal. It will destroy me."

Drawing her chin up, he met her gaze. "Whatever you've heard about me, whatever may have been said, it wasn't true, Lila. I never gave you any reason to turn to Chris."

Every quivering nerve wanted to believe him, wanted to cast aside the barriers her mind raised and give into the sweet sensation of being held in his arms once again.

"You never gave me any reason not to."

He ran a hand through the thick blond hair at the back of his head. "What you experienced is no different from what any other hockey wife goes through. You've blown it out of proportion."

Sucking in a shocked breath, Lila could only stare up at his hard, frustrated features.

What was it she was exaggerating? The loneliness? The infidelity? The feeling of being in a part-time marriage and still coming in second to her husband's career?

Pushing past him, she said, "You've proved my point, Cahal. I can't go through with this. I can't keep making the same mistakes."

Nearly out of the door, his voice stopped her.

"Our marriage wasn't a mistake, Lila. I'll prove that to you yet."

*

A perusal of the official Internet site devoted to the team told her that while the rest of the players were touring, Jack Jarrett and another player were left behind in Toronto. The other player was recovering from knee surgery but Jack was listed as a healthy scratch, meaning that while he was physically able to play he was not going to be utilized by the team's coach.

They agreed to meet at a downtown restaurant; Lila agreed with a measure of relief that he hadn't suggested something more private or intimate. Her husband's warning still echoed in her ear.

As she slid into the booth where Jack was already seated, she noted the lines in his face and the darkness beneath his eyes. If she were called upon to hazard a guess, she would have said he last slept several days ago.

He moved his blue eyes over her slender figure in its close-fitting black pants and colorful long sweater. "You look good."

"Thanks." She couldn't return the compliment.

Lila ordered a soft drink and made the pretense of reviewing the menu but Jack wasn't willing to wait.

"Are you going to tell me what this whole thing is about?"

Gone was the fury of the day before. He seemed willing to be convinced—of what, Lila wasn't entirely sure.

When she didn't immediately speak, he went on. "It's a publicity ploy, isn't it? Your faces were plastered everywhere overnight, Cahal Wallace and his cute little hometown gal. That has to be the real reason you went back with him."

His guess was surprisingly good. Sensing something was wrong with the lightning reconciliation, he sought the obvious solution.

Lila poked a finger through the largest hole. "Why would Cahal need more publicity?"

Jack took a leisurely swallow of his beer, his eyes still locked on her. "With those superstars, I heard there's no such thing as too much."

"That's money," she replied, "not celebrity. Most of your colleagues are good Canadian boys who don't care for notoriety."

"Notoriety is right," Jack murmured as the waitress made another pass around their table and managed to catch Lila's eye, dooming them to put in an order they didn't want and Lila knew she wouldn't be able to eat.

"I don't want to talk about Cahal," she said. "I wanted to talk about you and me, Jack."

He let the comment sink in for a full minute before he spoke, low and vehement. "Do you think I'm blind?"

She stared. "What? No!"

Jack went on as if she hadn't spoken.

"I know he managed to lure you back. What I want to know is how? Money? Promises of even greater stardom? What?"

The questions hit her like a barrage of hammer blows, shocking in their violence.

"I love him."

Her answer was a firm yet gentle counterpoint and it sounded believable even to her ears.

For a second Jack looked stunned until his quick reflexes brought him back up, fighting.

"And you didn't know this a few months ago when we started dating?"

"I knew it even then," Lila heard herself saying, "but I struggled to deny the truth. I should have known better than to go against what felt right and natural. I'm sorry, Jack. Really, I am."

"Sit down."

Lila hadn't risen, yet after speaking the perfect exit lines she was already sliding out of the booth. The command brought her feet back onto the edge of the raised floor and she unwillingly settled her bottom back into the tough upholstery.

"I'm sitting."

She owed him the courtesy of a ready ear.

He leaned forward over the high table. "You've got to help me."

"Help you?" Lila probably looked as blank as she sounded. "With what?"

Reaching into the pocket of his jacket, her companion threw a handful of crumpled papers down between them.

"This."

Lila moved reluctantly to take the balled up pages and smooth them out on the tabletop. They were all articles from newspapers, except for one that came from a glossy weekly sports magazine. All were pictures of Cahal and her, old shots from their days in Chicago, and all told the same story of tragic parting and triumphant reconciliation in the most glowing words imaginable.

Looking up from a particularly saccharine quote, she said, "That drivel didn't come from me. This hasn't been easy for me, Jack, and it certainly hasn't been a dream come true as this guy writes. It hurts me to hurt you."

Though she had already abandoned any hope of convincing him without words that she was doing this for both of them, she still wanted him to believe her in this at least.

"That's a load of bull!"

Jack's voice brought the anxious waitress within a few feet but one glance at his face kept her from coming any further.

"Keep your voice down," Lila hissed. The last thing they needed was some observer to grab his cell phone and take a quick picture of the newly reconciled Mrs. Cahal Wallace with her ex-boyfriend.

Jack's volume stayed turned up. "I'll keep my voice down when you explain all of this to me, this time without the crap. I don't believe you love him. He cheated on you. While he was keeping you sweet and pampered in his big house, he was fucking around behind your back. Tell me you love him still. Tell me."

The force of his anger hit her full in the face and she backed down from the humiliation of answering him in the way she needed to, admitting that she loved a man who could shame and disrespect her on a constant basis.

"He loves me," she said instead, "despite what he did and I need to give the marriage another try."

Dark eyes searched her face before jerking away. "Then you probably deserve the marriage you're in. Wallace is a cold, manipulative bastard, but he's got you right where he wants you and for some reason you're willing to make the same mistake twice. Just remember that I won't be waiting the next time he hurts you, ready to pick up the broken pieces."

Now she had nothing left. No marriage once the contract was over and no boyfriend.

"I won't need you to do that, Jack. You have to trust me that I know what I want finally."

He downed the rest of his beer in a gulp. "I don't know about what you want, but you're sure getting what you deserve."

Lila's patience was wearing thin.

"That's my decision, isn't it?"

Jack eyed her darkly. "You heartless bitch. I see right through your lies, just as I see right through your motives. I was never rich enough or successful enough."

Lila jumped to her feet at the first epithet and struggling into her coat couldn't help but hear the rest of his venom.

"You don't know the first thing about this situation," she told him in a low voice, "but you don't care to understand, do you? You only know that you're hurt and you want to hurt someone in return. Well, I'm not going to be your target."

"Sit down, Lila."

The belligerent command no longer worked and she was out of the booth and halfway across the restaurant before he had pulled out his wallet to settle the bill. A taxi was fortunately waiting outside of the door and she hopped into it with a confused order to take her to the apartment. She wanted to be in the safety of closed walls before she gave way to tears and disillusionment was always upsetting.

The future was growing bleaker by the day.

Chapter Seven

November days were cold even when the sun shone, and Lila traveled to and from work in darkness. Home life was depressingly repetitive. Rarely did she see Cahal although signs of his movements were evident in the debris he left. The condo suggested an intimacy that was impossible to form with inanimate objects.

The rambling Chicago house had allowed her to forget her husband's existence for days at a time. Out of the house and out of the city meant the same thing. The coach had believed in preserving his players' energy during stressful periods such as championship series and he often ordered the team to check into a hotel for several weeks even during home stretches.

The telephone rang with regularity.

"Hello, darling."

She suspected the phone line was tapped; otherwise his endearments were pointless.

"What do you want?" In the absence of an audience she didn't try to pretend.

Deep laughter rumbled in her ear. "Such affection."

Eyes fixed on the television she turned on for company in the evenings, Lila resisted the urge to throw the phone at the enormous screen.

"I'm not here to stroke your ego," she told him.

Cahal laughed again. "That's not the part that needs stroking."

As satisfying as it was to slam the phone down on his amused voice, she was forced to pick it up a moment later when his cell phone number displayed. This time he didn't bother with a greeting.

"This isn't a joke, Lila."

"Don't I know it," she sighed.

In the following silence, she could almost hear him counting to ten and probably swearing to himself. When he spoke, he sounded very calm and level.

"What are you doing?"

Lila stiffened up again. "Watching television."

"Anything good?"

"No."

His voice dipped lower. "I miss you."

She nearly dropped the phone. "Damn it, Cahal, what are you trying to prove?"

"I'm trying to be a good husband."

It was impossible to tell if he was joking, although it was the obvious conclusion.

"It's too late for that," she said. Angry tears sprang up, blurring the chaotic images onscreen. "In all the years we were married you never told me that you missed me."

Flowers and expensive presents never made up for his emotionless words over the phone. Daily calls were appreciated but most wives received those; Lila was the only one who could never quote a particularly soppy line from her husband because there weren't any. Always vague about the details of his own activities, Cahal wanted to know about every minute of her day even though the recitations were usually very dull.

"I'm telling you now," he replied in the same low tone.

"I don't want to hear it now! I wanted to hear it then."

Another series of rustles expressed his restlessness. "What do you want me to do? Turn back time?"

Deep breaths calmed her down somewhat. "No. What I want is a normal life."

"And you think you can have that with another hockey player?"

Lila sniffed. "I—"

He was right to be so caustic. She was hanging on to the familiar when the familiar was all that was wrong in her life. No matter what Jack promised for their future, their only hope for a happy relationship was if he retired.

"Baby—"

"No!" She nearly screamed out. "I don't want to rehash the past. We've done enough of that."

"When?" A smooth voice inquired. "You ran away and you're still—"

The phone provided a buffer. In person he would have been able to finish his sentences and she would have buckled.

"I'm not running," Lila cut in. "I'm here and as usual you're a thousand miles away. It's really like being married to you all over again."

"Lila—"

"I've got to go," she said. "It's getting late."

"All right." It was clear that he gave in to the limitations of the phone connection rather than her. "I'll talk to you tomorrow."

Lila put down the phone and burst into tears. Despite everything that had gone wrong, she still missed him. Damn him.

*

Lila's quiet workplace couldn't remain unaffected by the publicity machine Cahal's agent put into motion. The employee pool small enough to be cozy, yet its patronage large enough to be anonymous, the library was her last refuge. Now she never knew if the person on the other side of the counter wanted a rare book on special order or a few snapshots for the back of the sports section.

Complaints to Billy Avery's agency produced no reaction. Approaching the team with her irrelevant problems was unthinkable and, as usual, Cahal was AWOL. She was alone. Again.

On the telephone with her husband, she invented outings so that Cahal wouldn't worry. In reality she spent those weekends alone at the movie theater watching unpopular foreign films or at work doing after-hours inventory. The theater collected small steady revenue from her and the inventories had never been more up-to-date, but Lila's nerves were being shredded with every passing day. Counting down the hours until their ridiculous charade was over didn't help; she had nothing to go back to once the act was finished.

The library's employees had taken to cutting out articles about Cahal from the newspaper and tacking them up on the staff room bulletin board. Although the action was touching rather than malicious, Lila started avoiding the staff room and, increasingly, her fellow employees as well.

Teaching elementary school groups the basic tenets of research was usually one of her favorite duties but today she could take no pleasure in the small, well-scrubbed faces or the children's fidgety eagerness to begin their projects. After handing out the list of study topics, she paused to exchange a few words with the teacher, whom she knew from previous class trips.

The young woman broke off. "I think that man over there is trying to get your attention."

Lila looked across the short stacks of children's reference books. Tall. Blond. Muscular. From a distance it could be her husband, yet she never made that mistake.

Catching the teacher's curious look, Lila explained, purposely inaccurate, "He's a relative of mine visiting from out of town."

"Too bad he's a relative," the other woman murmured, obviously not recognizing the face which regularly appeared on advertising across the country. "What about an introduction?"

"I'll keep you in mind," Lila replied, crossing to the front circulation counter where Chris Wallace was standing.

"What are you doing here?"

"Not a very nice welcome," he observed, smiling down into her worried face.

He was right. Chris didn't deserve any of the anger she felt for her soon-to-be ex-spouse.

"I'm sorry. You surprised me."

He nodded with approval. "You're like me. You like to keep your work and your private life separate."

Lila grimaced, remembering some of the speculative articles she'd read about her marriage. "Whenever possible, yes."

Leaning a broad hand against the counter top, Chris remarked, "That's hard to do living in a fish bowl. This city is the unofficial hockey capital of the world."

"I know," she sighed, tucking a wayward strand of black hair behind her ear. "This was exactly what I wanted to avoid."

He gave her an odd look. "I heard you were back with Cahal."

The terms of the contract strangled any possibility of an explanation.

"Yes." She couldn't resist adding, "For now."

"Even Jarrett would have been better," Chris remarked, shoving his hands into the pockets of his leather jacket.

She stared at him. "Why?"

"For selfish reasons. Then I would still be able to see you." His hand reached for her face before he checked the movement in mid-air. "You've always been decent to me, even when I was just Cahal's younger cousin, wearing his cast-off equipment and living in his shadow."

It was surprising to hear this interpretation of the family dynamic. With both players forecasted for future superstardom by the time they entered the professionals, Cahal had reached this level first but Chris' outgoing personality and somewhat wild reputation assured him sponsorship deals and greater financial success. Cahal was still the star but Chris was more often the face on cereal boxes and commercials.

Yet, because Cahal had achieved success first, even turning around to hook Chris up with his first agent, Chris never stopped resenting his cousin. In hockey, youth was everything and Chris' grudge went a long way back to when Cahal was scouted as a very young child, leaving Chris to develop a talent that didn't shine until he had reached his early teens.

"If you were ever in his shadow, you've escaped it by now." Glancing around the library, she was conscious of the interested stares they were getting from her colleagues. "Chris, I have work to do right now."

"I'm in town for two days," he told her. "I have a guest spot on the Prime Time Sports show. How about dinner tonight? My hotel has a great restaurant attached to it."

"Your hotel?" The question slipped out, causing his expression to subtly alter.

"I can control myself," he assured her. "Put that night down to too much alcohol and too many painful revelations."

Though his voice was cool, his blue-blue eyes assessed her face. Lila flushed, remembering nothing of the night but with the pictures he'd taken on his phone vivid in her mind. Her nude body, laid out on the wide bed like a sacrificial offering, and Chris' hand hovering above it.

Why had he taken the pictures? She'd asked herself that a thousand times. But maybe men like Chris always took pictures. That was his trophy.

"Your hotel is fine," Lila said. "You can pick me up after work. I finish at five-thirty."

She didn't want him coming to Cahal's apartment, knowing that her husband wouldn't appreciate his cousin visiting in his absence.

"It's a date," Chris confirmed before striding out of the building, leaving before Lila could change her mind about the assignation.

Already she was regretting her recklessness.

*

Chris' truck might have cost the earth but it was still a pick-up, modest in looks and manufactured domestically. The utilitarian design was as deceptive as the man behind the wheel, the lack of ornamentation concealing powerful and undeniable ability.

"I saw you in a magazine last week. I think it was an ad for jeans."

Her companion cocked an eyebrow. "You think?"

The eyebrow made her unaccountably flustered.

"It was hard to tell." He was nearly naked in the ad, a pair of battered jeans being the only thing he wore. "You know how advertisements are these days."

He shrugged. "I guess I should. I'm in enough of them."

"Why?"

"Why am I in so many ads?"

Lila nodded.

He thought. "I suppose it's how my agent measures success. Any hockey player can sign a contract worth a million dollars a year. How many make more on their endorsements than they do playing the game? How many become household names? The more I earn, the more my agent earns and the more famous I become, the more famous he becomes. It's not the way Billy Avery thinks but it's the way sports is heading."

A half-forgotten fact resurfaced. "Billy Avery used to be your agent, too."

His look was cool. "When I just started in the league, yes." The chiseled jaw that had graced a series of razor ads years ago hardened. "He only agreed to represent me because my cousin talked him around. He didn't think I was going to be big enough to bother with but he didn't want to risk offending the great Cahal Wallace."

Lila thought it was kind of nice of Cahal to convince his much-admired sports agent to represent his younger cousin yet she recognized the grievance behind the statement. Loyalty to Cahal had caused his own parents to push him away and even though his presence was an uncomfortable reminder of her mistakes, Lila felt a duty to stand by him. She had committed the same mistake and she hadn't been ostracized.

Chris surrendered his keys to the waiting valet but she didn't fool herself that that was all he had to say on the subject of his cousin.

He bided his time, waiting until the end of the meal to mention her husband again.

"So how long is this reconciliation going to last?"

Hiding her distaste, Lila replied neutrally. "That's a rather cavalier attitude to someone else's future happiness."

Her companion dropped his bantering tone. "You're never going to be happy with him."

"You mean once a cheater, always a cheater? Remember that I'm one, too."

For an instant, Chris looked confused before a knowing smile spread across his lips. "That was one time," he stated. "Your husband's adultery spans the last decade."

"I wish someone had told me about it sometime during the past decade."

His look was searching. "I told you, didn't I?"

"After I cried on your shoulder. You felt sorry for me."

"I still do if you're back with my cousin."

She couldn't argue with him. Only a fool stayed with an adulterer.

"Can we talk about something else?"

"All right." He smiled and switched topics only by the slightest degree. "Why'd you break up with Jarrett?"

Lila sighed. "Don't tell me. You hate him too."

Blonde brows lowered over smoke-blue eyes. "Who else hates him? Oh, your erstwhile spouse. He was always possessive, wasn't he? It's the hallmark of the compulsive cheater."

"Hey," she protested. "Put like that, you make Cahal sound sick, not just...bad."

She wasn't quite convinced that he was bad; his cheating was likely a result of loneliness. As tough as it was for her to sit at home and wait for him, it was no doubt just as hard to be away from home for days or weeks at a time.

"He could be both," Chris insisted, warming to his topic. "The guys on my team who take advantage of puck bunnies—sorry, female fans—are pretty messed up themselves. Looking at some of those women, the young ones with poor self-esteem trying to please, it's almost criminal to think of using them for sex. The young players do it because they get their heads turned, it's their first taste of stardom, but once they start down that road it's difficult to stop."

Puck bunnies was the derogatory name hockey players called the groupies of their sport, young women who waited at every city for visiting teams or who stalked members of the home team on their own turf, just for the chance of offering their company for a night. A kind of feminine bedpost notching for the enlightened times, hockey wives shuddered at the mention of these women, knowing that some players did keep company with them. Indeed, some of these women in time became girlfriends and wives.

"You're a veteran member of the team, why don't you stop them?"

Her companion lifted his hands. "Hey, I'm not the coach or a captain. It's none of my business what the youngsters want to do. I stay out of the team politics."

With an attitude like that, it was no wonder he wasn't a captain or alternate captain even after nearly a decade on his team. Although goaltenders couldn't wear the captain's "C," Cahal was widely hailed as a league leader and mentor to younger players. He wouldn't throw up his hands and claim to be staying out of the 'politics'.

Lila smiled. "Just like you stay away from the puck bunnies?"

"I do," he replied. "Who knows what kind of diseases those women are crawling with?"

Her smile faded. "I got tested," she said, "like you suggested. The results were all negative."

"You're lucky."

"So are you," she pointed out, frowning. "Unless we used protection."

"We did. Why, do you remember?"

Her frown deepened as she shook her head. "I told you I was too out of it. I've never had a head for champagne."

Chris' voice dropped, becoming intimate. "I wish I'd known that before we went to bed together. I feel like I took advantage of you. Is that why you refused to have anything to do with me afterwards? You know, I'm different from my cousin. I would never hurt you the way Cahal did."

"You say that now," she said. "Given the chance, he would have said the same words a few years ago. Only time tells us those sorts of things."

"Hasn't time told you what sort of man I am?"

"I thought time told me what sort of man my husband was," Lila countered. Remembering Jack's fury, she added, "Maybe I'm a poor judge of character."

Chris let go of her hands. "Since you're back with my cousin, I won't argue that conclusion. So where is Cousin Cahal tonight? At practice? I'm surprised he let you out of your cage."

"Cahal's out of town. I thought you knew."

"I didn't but I should have guessed. Of course he would never allow you to have dinner with me after what happened between us last year."

"It's not a question of allowing me," Lila told him. "I'm not a prisoner and he's not a jail guard."

The smirk on his face said the opposite. "So when do you get to see your husband? At birthdays and on holidays? Probably not even then. He spends his holidays sucking up to the media and performing charity work, right? He doesn't even bother to earn some extra money."

"Like you?" Lila said and regretted it. Chris did his share of charity work in Los Angeles, where the management expected every player to serve the community as well as the bottom line.

When she first began volunteering for the Wives, it was with a view of sharing some of Cahal's obligations. Even if she was just sitting at his side during a charity-sponsored party, it was still one extra evening she had him with her. After a year or so, the volunteer work became a reward in itself, bringing her closer to the other hockey families and providing a challenging distraction from the lonely days and nights without Cahal.

She ran a restless hand through her hair, putting it into disarray, and stared at him from between the tousled strands.

"Why are we talking about this?"

"This is your life, Lila. This is your future."

No, she wanted to contradict him, this was not her life or her future. This was a charade and she was irritated that he thought so little of her that he believed she would go back to the soul-destroying relationship he had first warned her about.

"*My* life, *my* future," she emphasized.

"So 'back off, Chris'?"

"You said it, not me."

They grinned at each other over their empty coffee cups. After Chris signaled the hovering waiter and paid the bill, he drove her back to the apartment.

"When can I see you again?"

Avoiding his eyes, Lila unclasped her seatbelt. "I thought you were busy with the taping of your show."

Chris' hands remained on the steering wheel. "This time, yeah. But I can always make a special trip."

Feeling his glance, she continued to stare out of the windshield. "I don't see the point."

"No?" For a moment, his voice held a husky undertone that reminded her of her husband. "We would be dynamite together."

Inwardly debating whether to end the conversation through an expedient exit, Lila wanted to remain to make her point. Like it or not, Cahal and Chris were family and they would have to work out their differences sooner or later. After she was physically gone, she didn't want her memory to stand in the way.

She turned her head just enough to meet his gaze. "Unfortunately, we know how we are together. One of us simply doesn't remember."

Though his blue eyes slid away from hers, his tone was jaunty. "All the more reason for us to try again."

Irritation hardened her clear features. "Chris, let me get this straight for the first and last time. That night was a mistake. I was wrong to lean on you and I was wrong to think I could get back at Cahal by acting the way he had acted. Sleeping with you didn't make me feel strong or glad; it made me feel weak and mean." Taking a hitching breath, she ground her meaning home. "If I had one wish, it would be to take that night back."

Hurt mingled with shock. "You can't mean that."

"I can and I do. I lowered myself to Cahal's level. I compromised my integrity and yours."

A big hand lifted off of the steering wheel, coming to cover hers as they lay in her lap.

"How can I compromise my integrity by sleeping with the woman I love?"

The suspicion that had been crouching in the back of her thoughts since that night with Cahal, waiting for a chance to spring, leaped into sudden action.

"Love?" She repeated the word, tasting it and finding it alien and distasteful in this context.

His fingers tensed over hers; his expression was far from his usual control. "I shouldn't have said that."

She'd never seen him look so unguarded—not even on that night a year ago. "Do you mean it?"

Again his eyes skittered away. "Look, can we forget it?"

"Chris..."

He lifted his hand and raised his head to show her a familiar face, good-humored and self-mocking.

"Leave it, okay, Lila?"

Her hand fumbled with the door, the cold air touching her face like a welcomed caress. "Okay. I'll see you."

He smiled as she stepped out of the truck. "You can bet on it."

Chapter Eight

Lila didn't mention his cousin's visit to her husband yet she found herself trying to make up for the omission in a dozen little ways. She went to team practices, chatting with the other wives and admiring their children. Taking on a greater role in the charity gala gave her excuses to be away from the house when Cahal was home.

She posed for several hundred photographs with Cahal, all set against the background of their condo, decorated for the holiday season. A few of the photographs would accompany the team's holiday publicity packages and one of them would be used for the upcoming calendar: the perfect hockey family celebrating the happiest season of the year. Perhaps next year, one of the photographer's assistants hinted, there would be a little Wallace to complete the picture.

Although she spent most of her time away from work watching her husband play or pose, she managed to avoid any conversation more intimate than a coordination of their respective schedules.

When the phone calls began, Cahal was on the road so she put the matter in the hands of the security staff he had hired. As long as they were going to follow her every day to work and back and even to the grocery store, she might as well utilize their services. Her husband made it clear that they wouldn't be dismissed and experience showed her that they couldn't be avoided though she was surprised at her bodyguards' discretion. Despite her fears, no one told Cahal about Chris.

Chris had called a few times in the week since his visit but Lila was always conveniently unavailable.

Lila's cell phone went off in her purse and she dug it out only to grimace at the tiny display.

"Another unknown caller?"

Nodding, she surrendered the phone to the man in the back seat of the SUV. To her astonishment, he flipped open the cell phone and held it to his ear.

"Who is this?"

Lila could hear no response to the harsh question.

The bodyguard's voice dropped lower. "Listen, lady, this is a dangerous game you're playing. If you know what's good for you, you'll end it right here before it turns out bad for everyone concerned. Especially you."

Again there seemed to be no response but the man snapped the phone shut with a satisfied expression.

Lila swiveled as far as her seat belt would allow. "Do you think it was her?"

"Has to be," the man replied. "But she didn't hang on long enough for a trace."

"You're monitoring my phone calls?"

It was the driver who answered. "Yes, ma'am. Those were your husband's orders."

Lila crossed her arms over the front of her coat. "I'm still not convinced it's Victoria."

"You don't have to be convinced," the man told her. "Your husband is convinced enough for both of you."

*

"Hey, baby."

"Hi." Lila allowed the kiss her husband pressed against her closed mouth but she made no move to return it.

He swept his eyes over her shuttered face. "What's the matter?"

Conscious of the constant traffic of his teammates around them, Lila said, "Nothing."

"Tell me."

She shrugged. "Your security guys can fill you in."

Taking her by the shoulders, he drew her into a quiet corner. "Did you receive another phone call?"

Lila nodded, the concern in his voice making her emotional.

He drew her close and the strong comfort of his body eased some of her tension. "I'm so sorry, darling. Instead of sending her a message, our reconciliation seems to have caused Victoria to switch her tactics."

Lila sniffed. "I still don't think she's dangerous."

There was less conviction in her words than when she had made the same statement several weeks ago. The kind of person who could spend time making a half dozen phone calls every day to someone who wanted nothing to do with her made her uneasy.

"If her focus is you, she's dangerous enough," Cahal commented. He paused for a full minute before saying, "I saw her at the game last night."

Lila drew away from his comforting shelter. "Last night? In Buffalo?"

"Yeah." His eyes focused on a spot above her head. "As far as I know, it's the first time she's followed the team on the road. According to our security detail, she's attended every home game the team has played and all of the practices that happen to be open to the public. I've filed for a restraining order."

It was an outcome she knew he had tried to avoid. A court case would mean publicity of the kind Cahal hated, salacious and career defining in the worst possible sense.

"I'm sorry." The mention of a restraining order brought home the seriousness of his situation. Their situation.

"This restraining order will cover you as well." His gaze found her again and a tight frown marred his beautiful mouth. "I shouldn't have gotten you involved."

"It was a less painful solution," Lila recalled, finding herself justifying his actions. "If it had worked and Victoria had returned to Chicago, everyone would have been happy."

"Then you would be free to marry Jarrett."

In spite of the surge of unwilling sympathy, Lila clamped her lips down against informing him of the true circumstances of her relationship with Jack Jarrett. The other man's ghost was still an effective wall against her tumultuous feelings for her husband and with few defenses left, she was forced to cling to that one.

Cahal watched her face closely as he added, "Or Chris."

Lila flushed, calling herself every kind of fool for believing she could hide anything from him.

"You were right about your cousin."

The frown deepened into a grimace. "Believe me, that offers no comfort. What happened?"

But Lila merely shook her head. She wasn't ready to tell that story quite yet.

"What happens with the security detail now?"

He accepted the change in topic with a narrowed look. "Nothing. They stay in place until Victoria leaves."

"Or until you get that restraining order," she suggested, anxious to call off the bodyguards dogging her every move. The feeling of being shadowed everywhere she went was almost as bad as the idea of Victoria Brantford lurking in the bushes.

A swift shake of the head dashed her hopes. "No doubt the local police are efficient but they can always use a helping hand to enforce the court's measures. Better to err on the side of caution."

Someone in the distance called his name.

"I have to go now. Stay with Brian and Mike."

She accepted another kiss, this one aimed at her forehead. "Like I have a choice."

*

Cahal wanted her to stay with his father, three hours west of the city, but Lila had no intention of interrupting George Wallace's life with his new spouse and children and she doubted that George would be eager to put his family in harm's way.

Lila remained in the city, forming a solid nucleus around which her husband and his hired security guards circled like uncertain moths.

The anonymous calls ceased but, of course, they had seized her cellular phone, presenting her with a new one the next day. Though it was state-of-the-art and slim enough to slide into the front of a pair of jeans, no one had thought of loading her old saved phone numbers into the new phone and Lila spent a painstaking hour doing just that, her old address book in one hand and an instruction manual for the new cell phone in the other.

She left Jack's number off of the new phone.

Lila took on all of the overtime the library could offer and heading into the Christmas season, with stories and signings and the annual visit from Santa to be organized, there was plenty of work. The evenings and weekends stretched out longer. The library offered those shifts to part-time employees, retired people and students, and Lila couldn't infringe on these schedules. Hanging around the library outside of her working time would be viewed as strange.

The only other outlet for her restless energy was the Wives and Girlfriends where Cathy and other women greeted her.

Lila couldn't fault the women for being suspicious. Aside from her sudden switch in roles, from Jack Jarrett's girlfriend to Cahal Wallace's wife, she was also guilty of being the spouse of the highest paid and most famous member of the team, a position guaranteed to create some amount of turmoil and jealousy.

*

"What about the marketing of the party?" someone asked, taking advantage of Cathy's brief silence. "Are we doing a radio campaign or television commercials as well?"

Everyone looked at Lila.

"Well," she said, "in Chicago we always sold out with a good solid radio campaign and some Internet and print advertising on the official websites and so on. Of course, the radio campaign should include every one of the players doing a guest appearance on at least one of the local shows, preferably during the morning hour. Most people pay the greatest attention to those shows."

The women swiveled their heads to look back to Cathy.

"That sounds like a good idea," the blonde woman agreed. "We don't have the budget for a television campaign. But are Internet ads necessary?"

"Not ads," Lila corrected. "Announcements on the local community websites and on the team's official site as well as the individual players' websites. The key is not to go overboard. This event is still fairly select—the prices we charge for the dinner itself is mostly out of the average fan's price range—and we want to keep up that aura of exclusivity."

Cathy's brows arched. "Oh, do we?"

Knowing how these groups worked, Lila backed down. "That is, I thought you mentioned something like that when we spoke the other day, Cath. It made a lot of sense."

The other woman again took firm control of the meeting. With the last of the jobs delegated among the spouses, the only issue to be determined was the prizes to be given out.

"A date is still a great hook," one of the women suggested. "What's a bigger draw than a private dinner *a deux* with one of the most famous athletes in the world?"

"They should come home to see one of our family dinners," another wife muttered. "Four kids, one of them invariably sick, a dog-tired husband and an exciting menu of tuna casserole and frozen vegetables."

"You know, you can cook those vegetables before you serve them," Nadia Ivanov laughed before turning back to the first woman. "I agree with Diane. A bachelor auction may be impossible with our team list, but one date wouldn't be offensive."

They were thinking, of course, of the team's owners, the ultimate arbitrators of any decision concerning the franchise.

"One date is fine." Cathy made the final decision. "But with which player?"

The women ran down the line-up. An amazing twenty-five players were married. Another handful were living in common-law unions or in long-term relationships with their girlfriends.

"Two players?" The wives were incredulous. "That's all we have to work with?"

The two names weren't very promising either.

"Karpetsky is an antisocial troll," Nadia pronounced. "He wouldn't agree to take part in a million years and even if he did, we would probably end up having to give the poor woman who won her money back once the date was finished."

"That leaves...uh...Jack Jarrett."

Most of the women made a desperate attempt to fix their eyes on something other than Lila.

Forcing a laugh, she said, "Don't rule him out on my account. Why don't we ask Jack to participate? I know he won't turn down a charity."

"He is attractive," Cathy mused aloud, "in a rugged outdoorsy kind of way. Not gorgeous but definitely not the worst the team has to offer. He's popular—"

"With the male fans," someone else pointed out.

"And he stays out of trouble off the ice," Cathy finished.

"Except for this latest predicament" must have been the unspoken addition each woman made to herself, although the media with its characteristic fickleness had failed to play up that angle of Cahal Wallace's reconciliation with his wife. On the sports and gossip pages, the story was a mixture between a fairy tale and a romantic film with no hint of soap opera melodrama.

As the final decision was made to name Jack Jarrett as the headline attraction of the Christmas charity event, Lila's new cell phone rang.

She couldn't help switching it on, waiting to hear the familiar silence that signaled a crank call. When the bodyguard had handed it to her earlier, she hadn't even wanted to take it, afraid of the small electronic device as if it had the power to hurt her.

"Hello?"

Instead of static silence, dim shuffling sounds signaled an unknown listener on the other end. About to hang up, Lila heard her own name, repeated in a long drawn-out squeal, over and over again.

"Leave me alone!" she shouted before clicking the phone off and throwing it onto the chair beside her.

A new phone, a new number, yet it was the same old problem with a slight twist. The caller taunted her this time, perhaps mocking her need to switch numbers and highlighting the ease with which they had managed to track her down.

Everyone was staring.

"What's the matter?" Cathy asked in a creditably even tone. "Prank call?"

"Yes," Lila said.

The other woman moved closer as she reached for a glass on the low center table. "How long has that been going on?"

There seemed to be no harm in saying, "A few weeks."

"I've been getting them, too," Cathy shocked her by saying. "For the last few days at least. I think they're from that Victoria woman who came to our meeting two months ago. She...said things."

Lila's training at the hands of her bodyguards kicked into high gear. "What kind of things? Did she make any threats?"

Although the blonde woman nibbled on the end of a celery stick, it was obvious that the action was meant to be casual rather than being naturally so.

"Not really. Well, not specifically what you would call a threat. She said that we would be sorry for choosing you over her, that Cahal loved her and not you, and we would see the truth one day."

Cathy paused to put down the half-eaten crudité. "It's strange because she never said any names, just you and her and him but I was sure it was Victoria and the way she spoke about choosing one person over the other made it plain."

"Did you call the police?"

The other woman looked astonished. "The police? What for?"

"Those were threats, Cath, and you have a duty—"

Cathy Monahan spoke right over Lila. "I have a duty to mind my own business and I suggest you do the same. I'm not saying I wouldn't contact the police if I were in your shoes but I'm not. I don't want to antagonize the woman. I just called the phone company and told them to add the call block feature to my line. Next time Victoria calls, I'll just block her number."

Nadia was frowning. "The woman can call from anywhere," she pointed out. "A friend's phone, a pay phone, it doesn't matter. Blocking one number won't accomplish anything."

Neither would changing her phone number, as Lila could have told them.

Cathy smiled as if she had known it. "We've all met Victoria. She doesn't seem like the dangerous type to me. She's just a little depressed over losing her boyfriend and who wouldn't be in those circumstances?"

It was amazing to Lila to see how she could be painted as the home wrecker for reuniting with her own spouse.

"We've known Lila for months," Nadia commented, "and we don't know Victoria aside from one meeting. If we're choosing who to listen to and believe, then I'm going with Lila."

As childish as the statement was, Lila felt a surge of affection for the former gymnast. Her stance was satisfying clear.

"It's not a question of choosing sides," Cathy insisted, adding,

"Victoria's father is one of the owners of the Chicago team."

Nadia nodded. "Oh, now I get it. I suppose if she was the daughter of the Chicago team's janitor, you would be taking out a restraining order against her."

This time the other woman didn't offer a denial. For every hockey player, no matter how rich or famous, the owner of the team pulled the strings and with trades an ever-present possibility, you never knew what team you would be playing for next year.

Lila's cell phone buzzed again, the sound it made muted by the cushions of the chair it lay upon. The other women stared at it and then at her, waiting to see what she would do.

Unwilling to brand herself a coward, she took up the phone, treating it as if it contained a detonator ready to explode at any time.

Her shoulders relaxed when she saw that it was an incoming email rather than a telephone call. She clicked the phone off, not bothering to check who the message was from. Nothing important ever came through her personal email account.

"It's nothing," she told the waiting women. "It's not her."

While some members of the group made a determined effort to put matters back on casual footing, Nadia was still stuck on the previous topic.

"How is your husband treating this situation?" she asked of Lila. "I mean, instead of lying low, your faces have been plastered all over the city for the past several weeks. With a security threat such as a stalker to face, now may not be the best time to launch a publicity campaign."

It was difficult to explain that the publicity and the security issue were interwoven without admitting the truth about her marriage, something Lila found was hard to contemplate.

"I disagree," Cathy Monahan said. "I think the picture of a happily married couple could go a long way to convince an obsessed fan."

"It hasn't so far," her friend countered.

Nadia was right. Cahal's idea had failed. Victoria appeared to be spurred on by the publicity, angered by the false images Lila and Cahal presented to the world. Lila was afraid of what would happen once the story went public, as it was sure to do when Cahal's restraining order was disclosed.

"Well, I don't see what's so bad about a few phone calls," Cathy huffed. "The poor woman."

"The poor woman has gone to the trouble of getting my unlisted phone number," Lila informed her in a voice that let some of her anger show. "This is my second number in as many months and she managed to get this one in less than a day. Yes, Victoria Brantford is wealthy and comes from a powerful family. That also gives her unlimited time and resources to harass me."

Cathy's face twisted. "And you're just a poor little librarian from the wrong side of town, right? That's a lie. I read that you and Cahal Wallace grew up together. You had your claws in him from the minute he started making money and you don't even know how lucky you are?"

"Lucky how?" One of the other wives wanted to know.

The blonde woman flung the speaker an exasperated glance. "Lila's known her husband from since before he was rich and famous. She never had to deal with people calling her a gold-digger or a groupie. She never had to put up with the suspicions of family members and agents and even teammates who all wondered why she was with a hockey player—whether it was for the money or the man."

The speech made a mockery of everything Lila had been through during the course of her marriage, all of the arguments and sacrifices she was once ready to make for the sake of her husband's career.

"No," she said, "I only had to contend with my life being turned upside down after my marriage, with a husband who was never there and an empty house surrounding me."

"We all have to deal with that," Cathy told her.

Lila carefully got to her feet. "Maybe I'm not as good at dealing with the pressures of being a hockey wife. A teenage romance never prepared me for this life and in the end I couldn't take it."

A long silence was broken by Nadia's cool accented voice.

"But you did go back," she pointed out. "You decided that you would rather be with the man you love than without him."

Lila nearly choked on her answer. "Yes. Yes, I did."

The other woman's dark eyes were astute. "And now you are regretting your decision?"

Lila smiled. "What decision?"

*

She shouldn't have spoken, of course; she should have kept her mouth shut and taken Cathy Monahan's criticism. What did it matter anyway? Her marriage wasn't real and the decisions Cathy seemed to think she had made weren't permanent.

Shivering, Lila glanced again up and down the deserted street. Leaving the meeting early, she forgot to call for a ride until she was already walking up the driveway and rather than go back into the lionesses' den, she resigned herself to waiting outside for her bodyguards to pick her up.

The night was fine and clear, milder than the last few days and with no bracing winds to make the already low temperature feel even more frigid. Almost an autumnal night, in fact.

Pacing to keep the blood flowing, Lila reached the shrubbery at the end of the paved driveway for a second time when she saw the movement in the darkness. It was a quick furtive action but in the absence of any wind, she felt as well as heard it. The thick mesh of pine needles made a crisp rustling noise.

A cat, she told herself, or a raccoon. Nothing to panic over. Probably nothing at all.

Her phone buzzed impatiently and she almost screamed at the small sound. A few pounding heartbeats later, she expelled a breathy laugh in a rush. She was getting paranoid.

Fishing the cell phone out of the coat pocket she'd stowed it in after contacting her security guards, she saw that it was yet another email message. Two in one night. She was a popular girl.

Without nothing else to do, she logged into her email account and checked her messages. Both messages were from the same person yet the name was one she didn't recognize.

Lila knew the antivirus protocols and she was about to erase both messages unopened when she saw that they both contained the same tag line. Lila at the Wives. To most people the message would have made no sense but the use of her name made a strong shiver travel down her back. It couldn't be...

It was.

Two digital photographs, both taken within the past hour and emailed to her account. The pictures were of her. One taken perhaps a half-hour before through the window of Jennifer Efflin's living room showed Lila sitting in a group of well-dressed women, her face flushed and animated. Probably taken during the middle of the argument with Cathy.

The second photo showed Lila a bare minute ago, standing on the edge of the Efflins' driveway.

The rustling became thunderous. Or was that just her imagination?

If it wasn't her imagination, then it had to be a litter of cats or a gang of raccoons struggling to free themselves from the shrubs, struggling to get near her and...

Lila opened her mouth to scream just as the headlights swept through the cul de sac, illuminating her with a wash of light. A man was out of the vehicle before it slowed down, grabbing Lila and pushing her into the interior of the SUV.

"Who was that behind you?"

It was a foolish question, yet she answered anyway.

"I have no idea. Did you get a look at its face?"

The driver looked grim. "No luck. What about you, Mike?"

The other man had a phone to his ear. "I was busy rescuing the damsel. Could have been anyone from what I could see. Shapeless black clothes. Hood pulled over its head. Hard to say if it was a man or a woman."

"A tall woman," the driver suggested, "or a shortish man."

By this time, his colleague was busy giving a description similar to the one he had just uttered to someone on the other end of the phone. Seeing Lila's look, the driver explained.

"He's talking to the cops. We suspected something like this so we stayed in the area."

Remembering the interminable wait in the cold, Lila's teeth chattered. "It took you long enough!"

"Sorry. We didn't think—that is, this is a step up from the old pattern. We were all hoping it wouldn't escalate, your husband most of all."

Lila could have given him a few choice words on the subject of her husband but she kept her shivering lips closed. There was no point in railing against the inevitable. Cahal would always be a thousand miles away when she needed him and paid substitutes were not enough.

"Where are we going?" The street they were on didn't take them to the condominium.

"The police station," Mike said, snapping off his phone. "We'll need to give them your cell and you'll have to make a statement."

Lila slumped lower in her seat. "I didn't see anything."

"Not enough to lay criminal charges, perhaps," was the response. "But it's part of a pattern and this type of evidence can be used to get that restraining order. You just have to stay calm and tell the police the truth."

The first part was a great deal harder than the latter but she got through the interview by answering the questions asked of her and resisting embellishment. When her guards dropped her husband's name, the service she received could not have been better. The two police officers who took her statement escorted her out the station door with a promise to send her a copy of the typed report the very next day. Even Mike and Brian were impressed.

The bodyguards' presence in the building didn't help her sleep that night. The condo was first too cold and then too hot and finally just too creepy. Never home in the first place, the penthouse felt almost hostile and she thought of spending the night across town in the apartment she still rented with her modest salary. Cahal might have bought her services and an expensive cage to put her into but she needed the small bolthole to call her own just in case the condo became unbearable.

After two in the morning, Lila gave up. Shrugging into her robe, she walked toward the living room with the intention of calling her security detail and requesting a ride over to the old apartment, but on the way there she noticed a flash of light coming from beneath the door to Cahal's bedroom and her bare feet squeaked to a stop.

Lila's breath rushed from her lungs, yet no sound emerged. With vivid clarity, she recalled exactly where she had left the two-way radio—on the bedside table next to her glass of water. Her feet would never carry her those few steps back to her bedroom.

A split second decision turned into a quicker movement. The knob was hardly in her hand before the door flung open and she confronted...nothing.

A ragged laugh emerged from her lips as she saw the lamp plugged in next to the enormous bed. The old promise. She'd almost forgotten.

Moving with none of her former hesitance, Lila picked up the small lamp glowing white in the dimness of the darkened room. A reluctant smile edged her mouth. For six years, that lamp had stood by her bed, dark and quiet whenever Cahal was home and reassuringly aglow when he was away. He'd given her the lamp as a wedding present. As long as it was lit, he'd told her, she would remember that he was somewhere loving her. Touched, she'd also thought the idea was a little silly—until he left for his first road trip a week later and she found the lamp on when she woke up in the half-empty bed. Then she had cried.

A day later, he was back in Chicago and life went on until the next time he left. That time she took comfort from the light he left burning and the separation was a tiny bit easier to bear. Again and again it had happened until she grew used to living life in day or week-long installments, to finishing conversations over the course of weeks. It became a part-time marriage to a part-time husband.

Shuddering, she put the lamp back, automatically reaching down to switch it off. Her hand halted midway. After six years, she found that she couldn't break the habit. Turning off the lamp was akin to jinxing her husband and hockey players were a superstitious lot, even if Cahal wasn't particularly so. In the end Lila decided it was better to leave the lamp on than to explain why she had turned it off and risk sounding as silly as the players who always laced up one skate before the other or who hopped over every line on the ice.

The big bed was a powerful temptation and without thinking too much about it, Lila hopped under the duvet and pulled the fluffy folds up to her chin. The last thing she saw as her eyelids drooped low was the comforting glow of the tiny lamp.

Chapter Nine

With the hearing scheduled for the following morning, Cahal was extremely calm. His team of lawyers no longer included the white-haired divorce attorney he'd previously thrown at her but a circle of youngish men with stiff smiles and a habit of laughing. The lawyers laughed often as Lila was introduced to them, making small jokes to which she had no idea how to respond. Even her husband seemed to merely tolerate their presence.

Over the dining table was spread a layer of statements and affidavits, one from each of Lila's bodyguards, and a copy of the police report she had filed a few days earlier. The meeting was long and repetitive and Cahal treated it with the same steely determination he displayed during games. At the end of the evening, the lawyers thanked him and a mostly silent Lila, and shut down their laptops and departed with hardly a titter. She gathered that it was not going to be the easiest case the young partners tackled and the knowledge of sure publicity would shine a spotlight on their efforts.

"This won't last," Cahal said, nodding at the silent telephone sitting at his elbow.

"I'm surprised the papers haven't picked it up already," Lila replied.

Her husband rose to his feet. "Terrence Brantford offered me a million dollars to drop the court application." A long pause gave her the opportunity to respond, something Lila couldn't have done with a gun to her head. "The money is for my inconvenience, as he put it."

A turn of his beautiful mouth made it clear what he thought of the offer.

"Isn't it too late to withdraw the case?" Lila asked the question, still unable to comprehend the dollar figure. "I mean, just the fact that the application was filed with the court is newsworthy information. It isn't the final outcome the public would be interested in—it's the spectacle of a hockey player and a team owner's daughter battling it out in the courts."

"You're right," Cahal said. "What else is new? You can tear your body up finishing a playoff series yet when it's over the fans only care if you win. It's your family who has to put up with your bad moods and recovery."

Lila set aside the glass of wine she'd been using to fortify herself following the lawyers' departures and looked up into his face.

"Is it that bad? You never complain."

"Whiners don't make it in the big leagues," he chanted.

She took a guess. "Is that one of your father's sayings?"

Cahal turned away. "My dad had a whole bunch of sayings about the big leagues. He never made it out of the minors."

Lila knew of George Wallace's own hockey dreams but she knew much more about the toll those dreams had taken on his son.

"Victoria's upbringing was the opposite of mine," Cahal said, when she joined him by the window. "She told me that her father expected nothing of her and her brother and they suffered no consequences for their failures. Everything she wanted, Terrence got for her."

Raised in the strict but loving household of her grandparents, Lila couldn't quite understand the deficiencies Cahal and others suffered although she once tried hard to comprehend. When her husband kept offering his own childhood as a reason to put off having children, she was patient with him. One day, she thought, he would come around. But then they ran out of days.

"Being spoiled must have been just as damaging as being driven to succeed," she suggested.

"It likely was. Victoria's brother ended up addicted to drugs and he stills spends a good portion of his time in and out of rehab facilities. She was promiscuous, living the lifestyle of a beautiful heiress and chasing after celebrity conquests."

Cut by the way he rattled off information about the other woman, Lila hid her hurt beneath a cool tone.

"Victoria didn't seem ditzy when I met her," she told him, "nor did she appear to be promiscuous."

A second too late, she realized how silly and pompous her speech sounded. Having met the other woman once, she could hardly draw conclusions. It bothered her that Cahal had spent so much time with the blonde woman and that his assertions were well-informed and reasoned.

"When I met her, Victoria was already in the process of making a big change in her life. She was fighting her father for more responsibility with the team—before that she had always held an honorary title on the payroll which allowed her to meet any new players who caught her interest—and she was distancing herself from her old crowd of rich wild partygoers."

It was difficult to relate the slender, elegant young woman in Cathy Monahan's living room with a spoiled celebrity-hungry vixen such as those often portrayed in magazines and low-budget reality shows.

"Although she was well on her way on her own steam, Victoria credited me with the changes in her life and she latched onto me as a kind of good luck charm. Knowing that I was separated, her father pushed the relationship—"

"And it's hard to say no to the man who signs your paychecks," Lila finished for him.

He scowled out of the window. "It's not about the money. It never was. In fact—"

The tantalizing opening went unfinished until she prompted, "In fact what?"

By turning his head, his profile became etched in the glass, cool and distant. With the living version in front of her, Lila felt no closer to the real man.

"In fact," he said, "Terrence and the other owners knew very well that I was willing to leave the team if an opportunity opened up in Toronto, even if it meant taking a pay cut. That was done against Billy's advice."

This was news to her, not about Billy Avery, but her husband's willingness to sacrifice his career opportunities for a trade to the city where Lila wanted to live.

"W-when did you tell him that?"

"Before we were married. I knew you wanted to stay in Toronto with your grandparents."

"You never told me you requested a trade," she said.

He hardened both his real and reflected mouths into a rocky line. "It didn't come through so I didn't see the point in telling you. It made sense to start our marriage with both of us trying to make a go of it in Chicago."

And to let her keep thinking that he didn't care that she wanted to stay in their hometown, apparently. Lila was both touched and annoyed and after a brief tussle, touched triumphed.

She touched his arm. "Thank you for trying."

Her hand dropped when he stared at it. "You don't think I should have kept it from you."

"No, you shouldn't have, but I'm glad you told me about Victoria and the restraining order and her father's offer."

His smile flashed. "So I'm getting better?"

"Every day." The words choked her.

The silence left by the succession of rustling papers and legal remarks could not be a comfortable one yet it was tranquil, the kind of peace they were never able to reach during the tumultuous years in Chicago.

Into the serene silence, Cahal spoke with sudden violence, ably contained but potent.

"Would it have helped if we had had the child you wanted?"

The child you wanted. Beneath the painful force of the question lay the bitter direction of his thoughts. It was still her baby, the child she came close to begging him to have. He never wanted a child.

With honest simplicity, she told him, "A child wouldn't have made a difference."

Not a child he didn't want. He would have come to resent such a child, something she couldn't have borne.

The face in the glass appeared more distant. "Would anything have made a difference?"

Sensing that he was at a low ebb, Lila tried to be sympathetic, though she dared not repeat the mistake of touching him.

"The solution wasn't going to come from outside, Cahal. It was between us all the time, waiting to push us apart like water trapped in a stone."

The portion of his mouth she could see was tightened into a warped line. "Water in stone. Was that part of your university education?"

Lila's head went back. In seven years, he'd never thrown her education back at her.

Out of a perverse need to show him how she benefited from a higher education, she took the time to struggle against her anger and reply in a normal tone.

"It's late and I'm working the opening shift tomorrow. Good luck in court."

Swift as a striking cobra, he caught her arm before she turned away.

"Lila, forgive me. That was inexcusable."

She kept her face averted. "I thought you were proud of my degree. You insisted on—"

"On putting it up on the living room wall where visitors could see it," he finished. "I am proud of you, my darling. Always."

While the words eased some of the hot fury in her chest, it couldn't obliterate the lingering shock. A new idea rose out of the tight uncomfortable feeling.

"Cahal, did you think that I was jealous of your career?"

"No."

The answer came a little too quickly.

Her fingers stilled in his grasp. "It makes sense now. You were always pushing my education, my degree, when your career made it impossible to work or do anything outside of the charity work the team arranged. Did you think it was all I had?"

The hand holding hers went tight and then let go.

"Outside of me, yes."

"Thanks." The word came on a stinging intake. "Thanks for letting me know how you feel."

He pinned her with his silver eyes. "You don't know the first thing about how I feel."

Lila turned back to the darkened lake, her perch on the top floor giving her a strange distant view of the nearby crescent-shaped island to which its inhabitants traveled from their jobs in the city. The island was disputed land; technically belonging to the city but rented out on long-term leases to the inhabitants who built houses, tended gardens and raised families on contract. Now the islanders wanted to the chance to buy the land they loved and the city wanted to turn it into an extension of the water park, demolishing houses and replacing them with roller coasters and gift shops.

Simple things—a piece of land, a home, yet there was a world of difference between the two.

She pressed her forehead against the cold glass.

It was true. It was all a matter of perspective. She didn't know how he felt, driving himself to the limits of his strength and endurance every day, spending half of his time far from home, any more than he understood what it was like to stay behind and wait for his return. Tending the garden and not knowing if she would be there to reap the harvest.

Her life had been lived on contract, dependent foremost on Cahal's security as the team's number one goaltender but also on his health, his popularity, the ability of the team to meet his salary commitments. Many teams in smaller cities simply could not afford a player of Cahal Wallace's caliber.

Hating herself for the weakness, she was contemplating heading down a path she already knew well and had reason to dread. Remembering how life had been in Chicago was also imagining what life would be again returning to a role Cahal never truly asked her to resume. Because he hadn't. He warned her about Jack and she recognized the reasoning behind his warning. He'd enlisted her help for another reason altogether. While he'd hinted about the past and their mistakes, he hadn't come out and asked her to be his wife for real.

"I have a job now," she said, her voice a soft fog against the cool glass. "I volunteer for local fundraisers. I help out with the Wives. I've been taking a course in ceramics at the community college. I'm busy. I don't spend all of my time sitting and waiting for you to come home or around people who only know me as your wife."

"That's good." The smoky reflections gave no hint of his facial expression.

"It is good," Lila agreed. "It's also lonely."

The admission landed between them.

Turning to meet his eyes, she went on. "It's good to step out of your shadow because I never realized just how large and suffocating it was until we separated. Even Chris, I think, never saw me as Lila, only as your wife."

The pieces fit together. Chris' sympathy, his obsession with her, his desire to snatch her away from his cousin and his later disinterest in winning her for himself—it all showed that he saw her as an extension of Cahal rather than a woman in her own right. Well, he was in good company.

"So you're happy to be free," her husband said.

Her vigorous nod hurt her neck.

"You also said it was lonely."

"Until a couple of months ago, I never thought it would be."

"Oh, yes, the boyfriend." He regarded her through narrowed eyes. "I forgot about the picket fence and the yard full of toys, just as you seem to have forgotten that he was a hockey player like me."

"His priorities were different."

It was clear he didn't like her quiet answer, for his eyes became a silver gleam through thick gold lashes.

"I guess that says it all." He pushed away from the window in a savage motion, pausing long enough to glance down at her glossy dark head. "By the way, it isn't too late for us to withdraw the case but I would never exchange your safety for money or a break from the publicity."

"*My* safety?" Lila tilted her head back. "But..."

"The restraining order names us both," he explained, "but it was your safety that mattered. If I was still the only target of Victoria's campaign I would have never considered going to the courts."

It took a moment for Lila to take this in. He was doing this for her. The time and expenses, the publicity that could destroy his career, the challenge against one of the team owners. While he had gotten her into this mess, he was going far beyond modest measures to extricate her.

"You always had an over-inflated sense of responsibility."

She was thinking of his parents and even Chris.

Cahal's smile was restrained. "You may be right. I'm leaving early in the morning for court so I'll see you tomorrow night."

Lila remained awake long after he was gone. All throughout the night, the messages rolled into her new phone. Each text message

was only two words in length, stark and to the point. *He's mine.*
He's mine. He's mine.

In the end, Lila was ready to agree with the other woman. Lila
was never able to give her husband what he needed.

*

The least respected of the city's three serious newspapers broke the
story the next day.

On her way to work, Lila saw the front page headline and nearly
turned back. It was bad enough that she was unable to accompany
Cahal to the courthouse for the first hearing; now her knowledge of
the events of her own life was no better than any member of the public.

The streetcar took her past the courthouse, a slim commercial-
type building aesthetically unsuited to the emotionally fraught
cases it handled. The lobby overflowed with reporters and for
an instant, Lila thought she saw her husband's broad-shouldered
lean-hipped figure within the crush of eager bodies. Closing her
eyes, she didn't open them again until her stop was announced.
The squat brown-brick library was a welcome sight.

During her morning break, she used one of the television sets
from the audio-visual department to check the local twenty-four
hour news channels. The scrolling ticker at the bottom of the
screen gave the same information each time: Toronto goaltender
Cahal Wallace in court today against alleged stalker.

The midday newscasts expanded the story. Every local news
station sent a reporter to the courthouse and each camera showed
a different angle on Cahal's clear features. Accustomed to cameras
and giving interviews at a young age, now he was silent, no doubt
warned by his lawyers not to speak to reporters about the case. The
lawyers' statements were curt. Mr. Wallace regretted the need for
such a step. Mr. Wallace hoped for a quick and effective judicial
determination.

The opposing lawyers spoke as well, calling the case a ruse and a publicity stunt. As if anyone would want to call that kind of publicity on themselves. The reporters said little about the alleged stalker, mentioning Victoria's name only once during the broadcast. As of four o'clock that afternoon, Cahal was still in court. He called twice, each time to say nothing more than he was still waiting, yet the fact that he was calling told her a great deal.

Lila learned the outcome of the long day in court from the evening news. Presumably Cahal was conversing with his lawyers or stuck in traffic. Or maybe he was just avoiding her. After eight hours in court, he came away as he went in…with nothing. Not a piece of paper protected him from Victoria Brantford's attentions.

The ultramodern condo was a steel-and-glass cage. While Victoria was free to wreak havoc on her life, Lila was forced to take shelter and hide. That workday had felt long with the phone ringing and having to pretend that she was someone else whenever she answered. She couldn't face the thought of another day like that, and another, and another.

Cahal came home at eight. He looked at her huddled figure on the couch and swept her into his arms. The television babbled nonsense as he kissed her sore eyelids, touched the pale curve of her cheek, and an annoying commercial jingle rang out as his lips met her mouth.

The kiss moved from comforting to explicit in seconds, the change leaving her frozen. Sensing the sudden withdrawal, Cahal drew back and she could see the lines of tension etched along the side of his mouth.

"Rough day?"

He smiled as he stroked her face. "It's getting better."

Though it threatened his beautiful smile, she had to ask, "What did Victoria have to say?"

The smile disappeared. "You mean what did her lawyers have to say? Mainly that I was a liar, followed by a blatant self-promoter who was willing to do anything to further his career and possibly a sociopath. At best, I was an adulterous fame-whore who led a poor fragile heiress to believe that I would leave my wife to marry her. Hell!"

The last curse was convincingly uttered, and Lila was forced to re-evaluate her thoughts.

Plunking down next to her on the couch, Cahal buried his face in his hands for a brief moment. "It was a nightmare, baby. My hotshot attorneys didn't stand a chance. The judge refused out of hand to make a single ruling until he saw more evidence."

Lila brightened. "You can get more evidence. What is the next court date?"

He told her the date. "There is no more evidence," he added. "The lawyers urged me to put my best foot forward for this hearing and we put everything we had in front of the judge. Both Brian and Mike took the stand. Victoria's testimony blew them away."

Uncomfortable with the mental image of the other woman perjuring herself for the courts, complete with bewildered tears, made Lila angry.

"Did you take the stand?"

He shook his head. "I couldn't. The judge ruled that because I had no direct knowledge of the incidents of alleged harassment that my testimony would be of no use to the court."

To Lila, the solution was simple.

"Why don't I testify?"

"No."

Ignoring the quiet explosion, she persisted. "I am the person at the center of this case. I am the one with the so-called direct knowledge of the harassing incidents and I am the one most affected by them. If I testify, the judge will have a fair chance to assess both sides of the situation."

"It's out of the question, Lila."

"The decision is not up to you," she pointed out. "I'll call the lawyers to find out if it's a good idea and then I'll come with you to court next time."

For a long time he was silent, his steel-gray stare fixed on his hands. Finally he said, "I refused to accept the suggestion when my lawyers first brought it up."

Stifling a burst of irritation, Lila asked, "When did they first bring it up?"

"When I filed the application for the restraining order."

"Cahal—"

"I told them the same thing I am going to tell you—it's too dangerous. I don't want you to become involved in this case any more than you are now. Victoria has already demonstrated her willingness to turn her anger and frustration on you. I don't want her to go any further down that road."

His intractable attitude made her want to shout yet she kept her voice thinly level. "Keeping quiet won't help to stop Victoria Brantford. You've tried to be reasonable and restrained every step of the way and every time we've had to step up our tactics to match hers. I won't stay out of the court case, Cahal. I can't."

A pair of long arms engulfed her and she was pulled into his strength.

"Baby..."

"Don't 'baby' me." Her voice was muffled by his suit jacket. "Sometimes I think you fail to realize that I'm not the teenager you first kissed."

"What is that supposed to mean?"

Lila shook her head, aware that she was costing herself the comfort of his embrace.

"Look at us, Cahal. We're different people from who we were six years ago and somehow we never noticed it."

His hands dropped. "Is that why you turned to Chris?"

Again her head moved negatively. "Chris was there to listen. He was...convenient." Drawing an unsteady breath, she told him,

"It was an enormous mistake, the worst I've ever made."

"Is that an apology?"

Gulping back a longer speech, she said, "Yes."

He studied her open face for a long time before rising to his feet. "I think I'll call it a night."

Lila's eyes went to the crystal clock on the iron mantle. "Already? You haven't eaten dinner."

"I'm not hungry."

Coming from a six-foot-four professional athlete, it was an amazing statement. She gaped at his back until it was out of sight. Far from healing old wounds, her apology seemed to have made everything worse.

Chapter Ten

Lila's testimony tipped the decision, forcing the judge hearing the case for the restraining order to grant one but only for her. According to the judge's ruling, not enough evidence existed to extend the restraining order to Cahal.

On the trip to the airport afterwards, Cahal declared the judgment a victory. His lawyers were more reserved. They warned Lila that the first few weeks of the order would be a test period to see whether Victoria Brantford complied with the ruling not to harass, annoy or molest. Their reserve stemmed from the fact that the judge had declined to specify a distance from which Victoria would have to keep away. Without that term, the restraining order was open to interpretation.

The lawyers spelled out that numerous telephone calls could be deemed harassment, particularly if they were for no reasonable purpose. But what about waiting outside of the building to speak to Lila? What about attending the same functions? The lawyers refused to give a firm answer to those questions, choosing to note that a final decision about a breach of the order would be up to the courts.

The team's latest road trip took them on a comprehensive tour of the western Canadian provinces and American states. Cahal would be gone for weeks. So added to the uncertainty of the order she'd just won, Lila was once again left to her own devices as the busy holiday season crept up on her.

December flew by in a busy rush. Many of her chores were familiar; writing up long lists of Christmas gifts, buying the necessary holiday cards and decorations, helping out with the annual toy drive at the library and the Wives' charity event, which was now scheduled for early in the New Year to coincide with the break given to the whole league for the Superstar Game. Added to her other responsibilities, Lila found that the Christmas tree and ornaments she had put up for the past five years in the Chicago house had gone missing during the move to Toronto and now she was forced to shop for new ones.

She settled on a mix of expensive gifts and cheap decorations. Next year, no doubt Cahal would want to decorate his home in holiday best but for now they only needed a bright show of festivity for any guests they might wish to invite back to the penthouse. With strict security measures still in place, the only person who saw the interior of Lila's apartment across town was the cleaner hired to dust and air the unit out every week.

George Wallace brought his new wife and their kids to visit in the middle of the month and Lila was nearly as excited as the children to tour Bloor Street and see all the shops and boutiques decked out for the holiday season. Cahal's half-brothers and half-sister, all under the age of six, were adorable though they ran amok in the flagship store of a national toy chain and made such a mess in the restaurant where they stopped for lunch that George felt obliged to double the tip the long-suffering waitress.

The visit ended with George and Cheryl begging Lila to spend a weekend up north with their family and while Lila made vague promises, everyone knew that she would not be keeping them. Without Cahal, she couldn't commit to any engagements anyway. As always, his schedule dictated their lives.

As the end of the team's road trip approached, Lila made an effort to slow down. The library owed her some vacation time and she arranged to take the days off at the end of the year. She needed the time to think.

Three months ago, her life was planned out in front of her, perhaps not exciting but the path ahead was comforting and peaceful. With Jack, she would have always come first. Yet, in all of the empty December days, she never once contemplated going back to Jack. He was firmly a part of her past.

She watched every one of Cahal's games on television, even the one game where the back-up goaltender handled her husband's duties. The team lost only one game out of the six they played.

Lila paid special attention to the breaks between periods when the players were often interviewed by waiting reporters, watching for Cahal. The Canadian journalists were conservative, sticking to questions about that night's game or the team's chances for remaining healthy—a crucial component of any winning team, for the injuries began to pile up starting from around midway through the season.

The American reporters were more outspoken. With all of the media attention in recent weeks, was Cahal's newly reconciled marriage suffering the strains? Would Mrs. Wallace be cheering him on during the Superstar game? The fact of his inclusion in the prestigious event was all but a foregone conclusion.

Answering the questions with a smile and a few words that could have meant almost anything, Cahal looked thinner and more hardened onscreen. Only the hungry glint in his steely eyes remained unchanged.

The restless look was intact when he arrived back home. With a series of home games ahead, he skipped all of the optional practices, spending most of his free time in the condo on the phone with his agent or on the computer checking his email. Lila was worried. Time with his agent inevitably meant trade talks and the emails could be anything from contract revisions to offers from other teams. Where was his next stop? Vancouver? Florida? Los Angeles? It was sure to be somewhere that would take him out of her life for good.

With each passing day, it felt to Lila as if a chance was slipping out of her fingers.

Talking to Cahal proved difficult. When he wasn't on the phone or the computer, he was in front of the television watching sports commentary shows, which were something he could never stand before. Meals forced them together, yet even then he was unresponsive to her conversational gambits, answering most in monosyllables and in such a way that made further discussion impossible.

He played his last game of the year on the same day Lila worked her final hours at the library.

Lila exited the library alone, the reporters having abandoned her story right after the court ruling. She nodded to Brian as she slipped into the front seat of the SUV.

"Where to, Mrs. Wallace?"

"Anywhere but here," Lila said.

The man refused to start the vehicle on such flimsy orders. "There's that party tonight at Dave Efflin's."

"Home then," she ordered, stifling a yawn. A long day at work followed by a longer evening wasn't her idea of a good start to her vacation. Of course Cahal and his teammates would have it harder with a grueling afternoon game behind them before they hit the evening's entertainment. It would be the last chance for the entire team to meet up before everyone went their separate ways for the holidays.

Thanking Brian, Lila made her way up to the condo and straight into the shower, shedding her clothes along the way. She wouldn't be surprised if Cahal returned just in time to change and head back out again after hoisting a few beers with the other players.

The waterproof radio she kept in the shower drowned out even the sound of water pelting out of the powerful nozzle. In the end, she felt more blistered than scrubbed, the hot water having awakened her nerves from their earlier exhaustion.

Wrapping a robe around her still wet body, Lila walked out of the bathroom still humming the song she'd just heard and collided with a solid figure.

Cahal's hands lashed out to steady her at the same time as his eyes drooped to the golden expanse of skin displayed by the robe's gaping neckline. With her arms imprisoned by his, she could no more straighten out the robe than she could push him away.

"You're home early," she observed.

Cahal's mouth quirked. "The game ended more than an hour ago."

"I thought you would want to spend some time with your friends on the team."

He raised an eyebrow, mocking this suggestion. "I see my teammates all the time. I would much rather spend time with you."

Swallowing a telling remark, Lila said, "We're supposed to be at the Efflins in a couple of hours."

He swooped his strong arms down to her wrists and up again to push aside the damp silk. Her blood began to beat loudly.

"I showered at the arena," he said. "It'll take me ten minutes to get ready. That leaves us with nearly two hours."

Again Lila swallowed. "For what?"

The flashing smile distracted her from his pounce. She was in his arms before she drew another breath and that was captured by his lips. His fingers caught in the damp patches in her robe, clinging, still it wasn't close enough.

His ardent heat leached the chill from her skin and she snuggled closer as he deepened the kiss to something wild and frenzied. Locked within her for far too long, the passion overflowed at the worst possible time, when her defenses, already weakened by stress and forced distance, were taken by surprise.

While her mind may have been confused, her senses knew exactly what was right—the feel of Cahal's mouth on hers, the hot sweep of his tongue, the firm grip of his hands against her naked flesh. Her only remaining protection was the thin robe lying between his surging grasp and her aching body.

Unable to check her lips as she was struggling to do with her body, Lila moaned his name low in her throat. Cahal's response was to crush her slim form to his much larger body, fitting them together, and as always, the contrasts between them satisfied a primitive female need. Even if the promise of his strength wasn't true, she yearned to hear it, over and over again.

This time she allowed the fantasy to consume her, knowing that it was false and wanting nothing more than to forget the lessons of the past. She made no demurral when he hoisted her up into strong arms and carried her to his bedroom or when he laid her down on the cool pale sheets and drew the silk robe from her aroused body.

Gray eyes glittered as he traced every revealed curve, drawing out the agony of anticipation until it became another siren sound of want like those already thrumming through the hidden parts of her body.

Lila ran her hands over the thick swell of muscle visible in his braced arms. "What are you doing?"

It was a soft meaningless question, a way to keep the want at bay for a moment longer.

Frowning, he answered her with perfect seriousness. "I'm memorizing you. In case this is the last."

Shutting her eyes, Lila refused to make sense of the words. It hurt her to know that he was torn with the same desperation, the same feeling of making love on the edge of a chasm that had just swallowed their marriage and their last chance for salvation. For both of them knew that this physical act, however beautiful, was not enough to hold them together.

"Lila."

She didn't realize she was crying until he caught her tears on his lips. But when he would have shifted away she held him to her with a single hand pressed in silent plea against his chest.

"Baby," his raspy voice was ragged, "what do you want?"

Her eyes opened, the wet lashes like the points of dark stars. "This."

She helped him to shed his clothes, letting some fall to the floor beside her and others to twist between the bed sheets, and stilled him when he would have come over her, needing to see all of him. The golden lines of his body were flawless, punished and honed to fierce perfection, his features mirroring that masculine savagery.

With tender trembling fingers, she traced every scar and welt, the faded reminders of injuries past adding to the beautiful whole. It was so long since last she touched him and a couple of the scars were new. Reaching up, she pressed a delicate kiss to an angry bruise at the base of his throat, marking the track of an errant hockey punk.

He watched her with a frustrated glitter.

"How could you do this with someone else?"

Lila didn't want to answer questions or even talk. When they talked, they ruined that perfect harmony their bodies could achieve.

With an impatient hand, she threaded her fingers through his thick golden hair, pulling his head down for a deep soul-drenching kiss. All of her pent up hurt and pain went into that feverish kiss but so too did all of the love she still held for this man, a strange concoction of innocent first adoration and mature love.

With no space left between them, there was no room for thought. Waves of sensation crashed over her as Cahal's hands felt every curve of her body, skimming the satiny skin at her hip, the silk of her shoulder, the warm pillowy softness of her breast. She ached for complete possession yet his fingers only teased, cupping her fullness, circling her nipple in a lazy tease. It amazed her that he could keep his wits when hers were fleeing, lost in the almost forgotten agony of the moment.

Gasping his name, she arched into his touch, causing his big hand to close over her breast. His thumb moved in gentle abrasion over her hardened tip, causing it to darken and swell, yearning for his possession.

Just when she thought she couldn't take it anymore, Cahal's golden head lowered to the nipple he had brought to eager life, taking it fully into his mouth. His lips tugged and pulled, his teeth nipping before he drew the engorged tip deep into his mouth and began to suckle. He did the same with the other breast, molding it first in his hand, then bringing it to his mouth so he could take his fill.

After an endless moment of mingled heaven and hell, Cahal's head lifted. He traced the path of his hand with his silvery gaze as it swept over her thighs and between them. She was hot and ready for him.

With a smothered groan, his mouth met hers, his tongue teasing a response matching his ferocity. As their tongues met and tangled with each other, he came over her, muscled limbs parting her slim thighs.

Lila broke the kiss as she felt him demanding entrance, her body unfurling to accommodate. Closing her eyes, she surrendered to the undertow, letting the primitive invasion swamp her.

Blind, nearly senseless, she used only her instincts as a guide as she met his thrusts with a rhythmic harmony. Rushing toward her was a powerful waterfall and she clung to Cahal's broad shoulders as if they were her lifeboat. All she knew was that when she went over that precipice, she wanted him next to her.

*

"We have to talk."

Ordinary words, yet they sounded ominous in his raspy voice.

Lila shifted onto her side, giving him a view of one golden shoulder he immediately took advantage of by running his palm over her exposed skin.

"What about?"

He tightened his fingers. "This doesn't have to be difficult, darling. In fact, this could be very simple."

She swallowed back a wretched sound. "I've apologized. I don't know what else to tell you."

Except that she needed him to do the same, without embellishment and coupled with a promise that he would never cheat again.

"I need to know what happened that night."

Flopping over, Lila buried her head in the pillow. "Except that," she groaned.

Far above her head, his voice was implacable. "I need to know."

"Why?" she grumbled. "I don't want to know about your women."

"There were no women," he told her for the thousandth time. With his hand, he cleared strands of hair from around her face. "Tell me, Lila. I can't stop picturing it and eventually it's going to drive me crazy."

Her throat tight, she asked, "How do you picture it?"

It was wrong of her to be curious but she very much wanted to know.

He moved his hand away. "Sympathy and a comforting shoulder, wine in front of the fire. I'm sure my cousin thought of everything. The Wallaces are very thorough."

"I don't think he planned it," Lila protested, "and it was very different from how you describe. The sympathy and comforting shoulder were there but the liquor of choice was champagne, straight up and only slightly chilled."

His breath fanned the nape of her neck. "I guess you never made it to the fireplace."

The place where they'd made love so many times. She shook her head.

"We talked and drank at the dining table, staring across at each other." Even the shoulder to cry on had been a figure of speech until the very end of the night. "I drank too much and when I nearly passed out in my chair I remember Chris carrying me up to the bedroom."

"Our bedroom?"

The graveled tone told her how much it cost him to ask the question.

"No, the guest bedroom." She closed her fingers over a hank of sheet and she watched them contract and release, contract and release, in a meaningless pattern. "Cahal, I wouldn't have—"

The same cold voice cut her off. "It's not a question of what you wouldn't have done. It's what you did. And what we're trying to do now."

It was about her, of course. It was always going to be about her failings, never about his.

As a hockey wife, she'd failed to be blind and when it was impossible to be blind, she'd failed to be credulous or forgiving, as the situation called for.

"What are we trying to do?"

Now her voice was as cold as his and it felt as if it came from a tight ugly place within.

She shook off the hand that came down across her shoulders. Screwing up her eyes tight, she managed to say the rest in a reasonably steady way.

"This isn't a prelude to a reconciliation, real or otherwise. This isn't the beginning of something new because a lot of time has gone by before we made this mistake once before. Nothing's changed. This is just sex. Basically, simply, sex."

For a long moment, there was a silence as complete as that which descended on an arena full of spectators who saw their team's hopes for advancement dashed with a single overtime goal. Then the mattress shifted beneath her and he was gone. His touch, his heat, his smell vanished.

Tears squeezed out from between her lashes. Everything she said was the truth. Why did she feel so awful?

*

House party rules mandated that the women and men stayed separate, the men gathered around the big screen television in the living room and the women in the kitchen. Children were banished upstairs where the Efflins' teenaged daughters kept the younger kids occupied. Every so often, a little one would wander downstairs in search of a parent, inevitably gravitating to the kitchen with its cozy warmth and aromas.

The atmosphere was festive with the little ones decked out in holiday hues and the adults in their semi-formal best. Lila's dark blue satin dress, low cut and flaring out just above her knee was tame compared to her hostess' gold lamé pantsuit, which clung like a glittering second skin or Nadia Ivanov's sleek red sheath. The men fared better in dress shirts and pants, a couple in suits, drinking single malt Scotch instead of the usual beer. The Efflins' liquor cabinet was more of an additional wing to the house and Lila lost count of the number of glasses of fruity red wine she drank.

Hunger forced the men to finally join their spouses in the kitchen where Jennifer Efflin's carefully prepared five-course meal became a stand-up affair with guests picking at blue cheese and endive salad and tender braised beef short ribs with their hands while the catering staff fluttered between them handing out plates and innumerable paper napkins.

When one of the husbands began feeding his wife morsels of spicy curled prawns, the rest followed his example. More than one woman ended up with a shrimp dropped down the front of her dress.

Cahal's blunt fingers made imperfect utensils. Lila blushed every time her lips came accidentally into contact with them. Her husband wasn't as shy. He laughed down at her with silvery eyes, making a show of circling her fingertips with an agile tongue, sucking every last remnant of sauce from them and often taking an entire digit into the scorching heat of his mouth.

After checking on the children, Jennifer Efflin suggested a new game. What about eating food off of other body parts? Husbands and wives only, of course.

The idea sparked the men's competitive instincts and incited interest in even the most hesitant of the women.

The caterers were left in the kitchen while the rest of the party retired to the Efflins' den, their host taking the precaution of locking the door.

Lila melted into a chair behind her husband's shoulder, hoping to avoid being called upon first to play. The tactic worked for it was Cathy Monahan who initially drew slips of paper out of the two bowls, selecting *caramel* and *leg*. Eddie Monahan dragged out the task of licking up the sugary sauce from his wife's calf while the rest of the men hollered for him to hurry up. Impatient for their own turns, none of the others wanted to linger on the spectacle.

Light-hearted jibes greeted each new couple who volunteered for a turn and compliments abounded when each task was completed, especially after the diminutive redhead married to one of the bigger defensemen chose *whipped cream* and *breast*. Although the male consensus was that the body part in question should be bared, the young woman only lowered her neckline an inch or so to allow her husband access. The defenseman made it clear that the game would be recreated better in the privacy of their home later that night.

Cathy Monahan looked all around the room with restless cornflower blue eyes.

"Who's left?"

Over Cahal's broad shoulder, Cathy's gaze met Lila's. The blonde woman's smile widened.

"Only goody two-shoes?"

The taunting question offered Lila an escape route but at the cost of her reputation. The rest of the couples had treated the game as light and harmless and after witnessing the PG nature of the interactions, she was less embarrassed. Every team had its vices—in Chicago, any couple who didn't play cards was unlikely to be invited out to parties—and judging from the ease at which the Toronto couples embraced Cathy's suggestion, this was probably not the first time that particular game had been played amongst them.

It was impossible to tell her husband's reaction from the slice of his profile Lila could see as she reached around him for the bowl.

She uncrumpled the first slip of paper. *Maple syrup.*

Lila wrinkled her nose. She hated the sticky feel of the country's national food although she loved the taste of it on fluffy buttermilk pancakes or drizzled over the top of a stack of crisp golden waffles.

Passing the first slip to her spouse Lila reached for the other bowl. She unwrapped and handed it to her husband.

Their hostess leaned across the low table. "Let's see."

Cahal displayed the second piece of paper in the curve of his hand.

"*Lips,*" Jennifer read out. "Nice."

"Easy," was Cathy Monahan's opinion.

It seemed to Lila that everyone in the room was staring at her mouth, her husband included.

"Where's the syrup?" Jennifer asked, getting down to business.

The small, carved bottle passed through several hands before it ended up in Lila's grasp. Her fingers curved around it.

"Come on," Cathy urged. "You've seen everyone else here do the exact same thing."

"Not the exact same thing," someone else piped up. "No one else got *lips*."

"I got *toe*," one man grumbled. "Whose lousy idea was that?"

"Ask Jenn. She's the mastermind."

A chorus of *shh's* shut the commentators up and all sound evaporated as every gaze swung to the couple at the center of the room. Lila was unaware of having moved, following her husband's lead to the spot where the others had completed their turns.

She wasn't flattered by the others' attention, for that evening was the first opportunity most of the women had had to ogle Toronto's newest team member at close range.

Far above her head, Cahal's smile was warm. "Our turn, I think."

"Cahal," she whispered his name.

He cupped her face with big rough hands, wrists meeting beneath the soft point of her chin. "I always forget how shy you are."

He spoke in a low voice and only she could see the shadow in his lowered eyes.

"She won't do it," a female voice said. "She's chicken."

"Come on, Lila," Nadia called. "We've all taken our turns. Don't ruin the game now."

Nadia's husband hushed her. "Stay quiet, honey. It's not as if there's any money riding on it."

"We should have placed bets," one of the men mused. "Wallace would have ended up paying through his teeth, which is only fitting since he gets paid a helluva lot more than the rest of us."

The competitive fire was sparked and soon everyone was placing bets on Lila's bravery.

Her husband's voice sounded in her ear, a throaty rumble. "You don't have to do it, love. Not if you don't want to."

Lila's eyes lifted. She knew what it cost him to be so nonchalant. He was as competitive as his teammates. More so.

She couldn't let him down. Not again.

Lila brought the bottle of syrup up to her waist and uncorked it. Silence fell as she placed a shaking finger into the mouth and raised it to her own lips, dabbing on the sticky liquid as she would apply lipstick. She didn't realize how seductive even that simple movement could be until she looked up again at her husband and saw the way his eyelids had dropped to hide a hungry glitter.

The surrounding silence took on a new depth as breaths quickened and hands slipped together.

Lila's sticky hand fell. The others' anticipation crept through her and tempted as she was to cleanse her smeared lips with her tongue, she wanted Cahal to perform the task for her.

He moved his fair head with the same determined strength she'd seen him exhibit a thousand times on the ice. As she held her breath, his lips parted to taste her honeyed mouth, first with care and then with hunger, as if he meant to drink her whole.

Syrup was still thick on her mouth when he cupped her head in his hands, angling it to meet the ferocity of his assault. Far from quenching his passion, the memory of their earlier intimacy seemed to fuel him further. The game and their audience were forgotten. All that existed was his mouth and hers and their struggle to be merged.

A tiny shift in the world around, a mere scratch of noise, brought Lila back first and her slow resistance forced him to surface.

Their hostess spoke into the resulting gap. "Wow." Her eyes were round. "I've never seen anything like that off of a movie screen."

Her husband let out a loud woof. "That was certainly something I'm glad I didn't miss."

Jenn Efflin cleared her throat. "I think we have a winner."

Cahal held Lila for an endless moment and when she finally lifted her head it was to survey an empty room.

"Where did everyone go?"

"To the living room for drinks."

Lila flickered her eyelashes. "I've had enough to drink tonight."

"Do you want to leave?"

"Yes." She wanted to end the evening as she began it: in her husband's bed.

Cahal's mouth curved. "I can have us home in fifteen minutes flat."

It took him twelve.

Chapter Eleven

A stream of limousines ejected passengers out onto the frozen sidewalk where men in stiff uniforms, nearly indistinguishable from the tuxedoed guests, ushered each chilled couple indoors.

The brown-and-gold lobby of the hotel was unchanged, its furnishings formal and subdued. A few of the regular guests gaped at the newcomers in their fancy clothes, recognizing faces from newspapers and Saturday night television. The constant flash of cameras and innumerable loitering bodies combined for a spectacle that made Lila light headed.

"This way," a young woman in the hotel uniform guided them.

Small signposts lined the way to the main ballroom where the photographers would be only those pre-approved by the team and charity. The hotel colors gave way to a predominance of blue and silver, the Toronto colors flying high in every corner of the massive room. Tiny team pennants graced the centerpiece of each of the eighty tables.

"Eight hundred guests," Lila murmured as she did rapid calculations in her head. Each ticket cost a thousand dollars and every ticket had sold. The overhead was not to be laughed at; the venue was the best in the city and the entertainment and food matched it, although some of this was donated. "The cancer foundation should come away with a quarter million dollars."

This figure spilled into Cathy Monahan's ear as they passed her table. The blonde woman was beaming.

"That's leaving out private donations made tonight, the auction and proceeds from the sale of any merchandise," Cathy said by way of a greeting. "If we're lucky we might reach three hundred grand."

Lila, who had produced similar events in the past, suspected that more than a hundred thousand could be raised through the auction alone. Perhaps more. The room was filled with the city's economic elite. These were people who wouldn't hesitate to spend dearly for autographed equipment or a day with their favorite hockey player.

The other woman stared at Lila. "That's a nice dress," she said with some reluctance. "Great color."

Lila's gown of startling winter white was unique among the crowds of black, gold and the occasional crimson or sapphire dress. The color played off of her raven hair, pulled away from her face, and smooth golden skin. A single shoulder upon which her husband's hand rested was left bare.

"I like your dress, too," Lila responded.

Cathy nodded in the direction of a nearby table. "That woman over there is wearing the same one in beige."

As this was undeniably the case, Lila could only say, "I like it better in black."

By silent assent, they turned their attention to their husbands' conversation.

"Terrence Brantford sent a big check along with his regrets," Ed Monahan was telling Cahal. "Twenty grand toward the cause."

"That's good of him," was Cahal's comment. "Whose idea was it to invite the owner of a rival team?"

Although each team's charitable events were not officially off limits to players or owners of other teams, an unwritten rule kept each team's endeavors restricted to their own cities.

The man averted his eyes. "I can't rightly remember. It could have been mine."

His wife's voice rose above the unconvincing statement. "It was my idea," she said. "After all the bad press his daughter created for our team I thought it was only right that he should give something back to this city."

Lila looked into her husband's eyes and she suspected that he was thinking the same thought. Twenty thousand dollars was considerably less expensive than the payoff Brantford previously offered. But no one would ever know that.

"Interesting crowd," her husband commented when they finally arrived at their table near the front of the room. He spoke in a dry tone, having already been accosted by a clutch of wealthy autograph seekers who all expressed disappointment at the fact that their hero couldn't give away for free what was going to be put up on auction later that night.

"Have you seen your agent yet?"

Cahal shook his head. "He couldn't make it tonight. He gave his ticket to one of his clients."

"Does Billy represent other sports?"

Again the answer was in the negative.

Since all of the Toronto teammates were coerced into attendance, without any reduction on the price of their tickets even though it was a working night for many, the ticket could only have gone to a member of a rival hockey team.

"You don't think it was...?"

A hard silver glitter came into his eyes. "He said client, not former client."

From that point, it was impossible to keep from sweeping the room in search of a familiar figure.

He arrived late, of course, when dinner was just being served and Lila had long stopped looking for him. He made his way through the tables, stopping at several to exchange a word or two. Nearly everyone seemed to know him but judging from the stiff smiles and curt handshakes not many liked him.

Lila's breath caught as he slowed next to her seat. He dropped a bruised hand to the back of her chair and it was pushed away by another. The buzzing conversation around them grew louder.

"Why, cousin!" Chris' voice carried across the room. "Don't

tell me you begrudge me a quick word with my best girl."

The words were as good as a battle cry and Lila felt every muscle in her husband's tall tuxedoed figure stiffen.

"I don't begrudge you a damn thing, Chris," he ground out. "It was always the other way around."

The other man didn't like that, although he smiled through the sudden fire that leaped in his blue eyes.

His voice dropped to a conspiratorial murmur. "Why would I begrudge you something I've also had?"

In a deliberate movement, Cahal came to his feet. Seen next to each other, the two men were more than superficially alike. In a white tuxedo to match Lila's dress, Chris looked trendy and fashionable. Cahal's version in black was far more traditional yet he cut a dramatic figure, which somehow made the other man look lightweight.

"One night compared to the promise of a lifetime."

Chris' smirk reappeared.

"And a lifetime was how long exactly? Five years? Six?"

"It's still going," Lila's husband pointed out with an edge of menace.

The other man dropped a wink in Lila's direction. "That's because you don't know the truth."

"I've heard the truth," Cahal said.

He swerved his blue eyes to the woman by his side and a sudden reserve covered Chris' features.

"What did you tell him?"

"What I remember."

The frozen look disappeared. "Darling, did you have to? I thought that was private between you and me."

Lila's mouth tightened. "Stop it, Chris. Stop acting like a fool."

Another audacious wink. "I can't help what I am."

Cahal's hand grasped her upper arm she moved to her feet.

"No, I guess you can't help what you are," he told his cousin.

"You can help how you behave."

With that, he steered Lila toward the edge of the room where several couples were taking advantage of the slow tableside service to cross the dance floor to the strains of light jazz. She moved into her husband's arms with a chill of foreboding; she felt as if she was dancing with a man made of tempered steel.

"Did you enjoy that?"

Lila blinked up toward the glittering mesh of chandeliers; he was a dark blur above her.

Her voice shrank in her throat. "How can you ask me that?"

"Because you seemed to be enjoying yourself," he ground out. "I just wanted to know."

She fixed her eyes on a point behind his shoulder as her fingers dug into his jacket. "How could I enjoy myself this way? I'm not a monster."

"It's perfectly natural to want to be fought over."

"Then I must be unnatural."

They swayed in silence for a minute, moving in their restrained little circle. Spurred by the lack of food, several other couples joined the dance floor, among them Chris and a beautiful redhead Lila was fairly certain was attached to one of the other players. At one point Chris appeared to maneuver his partner into the other couple's path but a swift glide brought them out of the path of harm.

Lila was dizzy from more than the giddy movement.

"It's getting crowded," her husband said, leading them from the floor.

The salads were at the table when they arrived and in the midst of eating and chatting with their fellow diners, there was no chance to speak to each other. Beneath the cover of noise and laughter, it was easy to conceal the fact that their eyes never met and across the room, Chris' eyes barely left her. Lila felt every spoonful she took being monitored.

When she moved from the table it was ostensibly to powder her nose, but in reality to draw a free breath away from her husband's side. She bumped into a solid figure coming out of the washroom.

"Lila."

Ignoring the urgent look he gave her, she tried to push past. "Not now, Chris."

"Cahal sent me."

She stopped and turned. "What?"

Though she had taken a long time in the washroom, rinsing her face and then having to reapply all of her party makeup, she couldn't imagine that her husband would send his cousin to retrieve her.

"I'm fine," she said. "I just needed some air."

Chris' ironic eye went to the washroom door. "In there?"

Lila ignored the question. "What do you want, Chris? Why did my husband send you to get me?"

Instead of answering, he surveyed the hallway and pulled her into a secluded corner by the telephone desk. Though his touch made her skin crawl, she went with him. The constant traffic to both washrooms nearby made their location public.

"My cousin wanted me to come clean about something."

He looked extremely uncomfortable, his face red and mottled above a no longer crisp white tie, and she became curious.

"What *have* you been talking about?"

The uncomfortable look was supplanted by a more familiar sulk. "It's none of his business, of course, but he wanted to know about that night we spent together and..."

"Chris!" Her hand crept up to the large diamond pendant at her neck, a present from her husband for one of their anniversaries. "What did you tell him?"

The sordid details of that night were a memory she never wanted back. She was glad that she only remembered Cahal's glorious body and Cahal's lovemaking.

Her companion smirked. "Don't worry, I spared him the details. Come to think of it, I've spared you the details, haven't I? Don't you think it's time you learned the truth?"

Lila tossed her hair to cover her bare shoulder; she noticed that he kept looking at that curve of naked flesh.

"I told you, Chris, I don't want to know." She lowered her voice. "We had sex, that's all it was. Meaningless sex."

He fixed his blue eyes on a point just beyond her. "Twice," he said. "Once on the floor of the living room, in front of the fire, and then again, in the bed. The guest bed—you refused to go into the master bedroom."

She flinched, her shoulders meeting the cold wall.

"I don't want to hear this."

A sudden bark of laughter made her stiffen.

"What's so funny?"

"You," Chris snorted between guffaws. "Your innocence. Your belief in me. Everything."

The parade of women he'd painted slipping in and out of her husband's bed appeared before her. Had he lied about her husband? Cahal had always denied cheating but the way Chris explained it, all hockey players cheated. Most just didn't get caught. Cahal was just unlucky to have delivered the proof into his teammate's hands.

"Of course I've believed you," she murmured. "Why wouldn't I believe you?"

His shoulders moved beneath his white jacket. "Because I have every reason to lie, as my cousin has brought home to me several times in the past year. He said it again less than thirty minutes ago but you refused to listen. You've always taken Cahal's side against me."

Perhaps this was true. Chris was talented in his own right but commercial success hadn't diminished his habit of sulking and feeling slighted at the least remark.

"I'd take your side now," Lila told him, "but you have to tell me the truth. What is going on?"

Taking her hand, he led her still further into the hotel, toward a private waiting area rich with gilt and crystal with an air of disuse. He led her to one of the armchairs but she refused to surrender into the wealth of pillows.

Lila stood, arms crossed, waiting for an explanation.

Chris' gaze rested on a thin beautiful rug. "I lied about that night, the night we supposedly spent together. We didn't have sex. You passed out from the alcohol and I took you upstairs to your bed. I spent most of the night staring at you while I came up with, uh, the plan."

"The plan?" She unconsciously dug her fingers into her arms, making the question harsh. "What plan?"

He scratched behind one ear, ruffling his short hair into artful disarray. He still couldn't meet her eyes.

"The plan to tell you that we slept together, to get you away from *him* and make you open your eyes to reality."

"Reality," she repeated. A dim spark flared within her breast. "The stories you told me about Cahal's cheating, were they true?"

Lila stared up earnestly into Chris' blue eyes and his were the first to shift.

"Yeah, those were true. Your husband's got a reputation. Ask anyone in the league."

Lila would rather lead a parade around a rink in her bra and panties.

But she didn't have to ask, did she? She had the photos—and Cahal's incomplete explanation.

"Who?"

Her companion's pose against a matching armchair was a little too nonchalant. "Who what?"

She was struggling with the urge to hit him. "Who has Cahal cheated on me with? Do you know their names?"

"Names!" He hooted. "As if I would know the names of disposable puck bunnies."

The woman from the photograph hadn't looked like a puck bunny. On the contrary, she might have been a businesswoman—or a high price prostitute.

No, she wouldn't even allow herself those thoughts. Cahal, of all men, would never have to pay for the company of a woman.

"He went with those kinds of women?" Lila asked.

Chris nodded. "I got it straight from Brad Drummond's mouth."

Drummond was the Chicago teammate who shared a hotel room with her husband while they were on the road. The roommate was always considered the best authority on another player and often appealed to for inside stories by journalists hunting a scoop.

"Brad Drummond is hundreds of miles away," Lila said.

A reckless light entered his eyes. "Janet Parker isn't a hundred miles away or even one. She's back in the ballroom seated right next to her husband. She told someone who told someone else who told me that she had an affair with Cahal a few years ago. Nothing major."

Lila sat attempting to swallow this final piece of information. Her companion noted that while her features remained blank, her hands had clenched into little balls in her lap. It looked as if she might be drawing blood.

After a few minutes, she got her voice back under control.

"So which reality are you talking about?"

For the first time that evening she saw a glimpse of the Chris Wallace she knew, vulnerable and oversensitive. The man she'd tried to protect. What a joke.

"I'm talking about you and me, Lila. *Us.*"

The heated emphasis was lost on her.

"What about us?"

Searching her face, he apparently decided that he didn't care for what he saw.

"Forget it."

After a moment, she asked, "So is that it?"

"Yeah." The cocky attitude was back in full force. "I thought you might like to know what you ruined your marriage for."

"I know what I left my marriage for," she said, "and it wasn't that. The night we spent together—or didn't spend together—was only the last chapter in a struggling novel. The moment I found out about my husband's cheating was the beginning of the end. I should have known from the very start that I couldn't live with that kind of betrayal. I still can't."

Chris' fair head hung. "I guess you don't think too much better of what I did."

"That was a betrayal of a different sort," Lila acceded. "But one for which I don't think I can ever forgive you."

His face stark beneath the mellow lighting, her companion turned and walked briskly away. He didn't look back.

*

Lila went home with an armful of memorabilia from the silent auction and a rhythm drumming through her brain. *It's over. It's over. It's over.*

It was over. Her marriage and whatever threads of it she and Cahal had been holding on for the past few weeks without any reason. The reason for keeping up the charade had vanished back to Chicago. The ball was going to be their last night together. No, she thought, looking over at the pure hard profile of her husband in the driver's seat, this was their last night. It was still going on.

"That dinner didn't fill the holes in my bridgework," Cahal said into the dim interior, even that mild statement causing her body to jerk against the back of the seat. "Those charity affairs are always the same. What do you say to a quick run through the drive-in?"

"Sure," she said as the familiar sign came into view. Then, "I don't care."

He ordered for both of them, far more than she could eat, and as he retrieved the bag from the pickup window she saw the impersonal leer of the teenaged server. The kid probably saw all kinds of fancy dress at this hour of the night when the nightclubs discharged their bleary patrons onto the city streets.

Holding the greasy paper bag in one hand and Lila's slender waist in the other, Cahal somehow managed to get them both safely into the condo without mishap. The cheap fatty food and Lila's brilliant white dress remained at a safe distance from each other.

"Go change," her husband ordered, propelling her into the bedroom. "Then we'll eat and talk."

The last word was spoken on a note she didn't recognize, one of near anxiety...or was it excitement? Why would he be excited? Lila's depressed mind couldn't work its way around that essential question.

By the time she made it back to the living room, wrapped in her most worn robe, Cahal had devoured the greater part of his meal.

"Sorry."

She sat down with him on the floor with a brisk arrangement of folds and flounces. "For what?"

"For starting without you. I was starved. I feel like I haven't eaten a proper meal in a year."

Her eyes shifted beneath the intensity of his stare. "That's okay, I'm not really that hungry."

Polishing off the last of his double cheeseburger, her husband said, "Let's talk then."

Nibbling at a French fry—golden crisp and salty—gave her something to do.

"Can't it wait?"

But they were both settled down and she knew that it, whatever it was, wouldn't wait. Not tonight.

He wiped his mouth on a paper napkin and balled it up and threw it into the bag. Wariness replaced the former...restlessness... anticipation?

"No." He took her hand in a convulsive movement. "We've been living on borrowed time for the past week. With Victoria gone, the reason for our charade disappears. That particular complication no longer matters."

What about Janet Parker, she wanted to ask. What about *that* complication? She kept her lips shut on a mouthful of half-chewed potato.

"Knowing what you know now—," a quick silver glance, "—we can start again."

She swallowed. "Just like that?"

"Why not?"

It wasn't really a question, it was a statement of intention.

She withdrew her imprisoned hand.

"I can think of a few reasons," she said.

He shifted, uncertain for once of what to do with his dexterous limbs. "I think those reasons are rightfully mine and I choose not to exercise them. With counseling and—"

"We've been over this before." Her voice rose. "The mistakes we've made aren't the kind that can be counseled away."

"It's worth a try."

He was being too reasonable and it made her want to lash out.

Suddenly she remembered what Chris had said earlier. Cahal had sent him out to find her at the ball. Cahal knew. He obviously thought *she* needed counseling after what Chris did to her and he was willing to make the personal sacrifice of restarting their marriage—for real this time—if it could help her heal.

Lila searched the chiseled face and found a tenderness that could easily be either sympathy or pity.

"It won't work." She faltered. "I-I can't do it again. It was bad enough...pretending."

"Lila." In a swift fluid movement, he was standing over her, his face filling her field of vision. "Now that you know the truth, doesn't it make any difference?"

Slowly, she shook her head. Now that he knew, he pitied her. It made sense. She was tempted into self-pity.

"There's more to it than that."

Cahal straightened. "It's still just sex?"

He'd probably said the same thing to hundreds of women in dozens of hotel rooms. Just sex. She wanted to agree, to turn the lie into truth. But it wasn't just sex. With Cahal, it could never be.

Her eyes fell to the frayed hem of her robe. "It was more than just sex," she said, adding quickly, "but that's still not enough. A marriage needs more."

"If you want to talk about love..." he began.

He said the word with such cool distaste that she knew it was over. The discussion was finished. They could go over the same tired ground for the rest of the night but nothing he said could erase the memory of that cold voice and hard eyes.

"I don't want to talk about love," she told him in a voice that echoed his chilliness.

His features were more than cool, they were frozen with enmity. It was a look she knew from between the bars of his goaltender's helmet, of determination and defiance. A "vanquish or be vanquished" pose which seemed to work well against oncoming teams. She told herself that she was fortunate not to be either. He would not destroy her, only the depths within her, flattening them so that never again would she hate so strong or love so fierce.

"I'm sorry," she said. But it didn't mean anything either. "I can be gone in an hour. I'll pack a few things and you can send the rest later. I've still got my apartment."

And her life. She still had a life...of sorts.

Beneath the frozen mask, the face she had known and loved struggled. He stood suddenly; unlike her, he'd taken the time to change into jeans and dressed, he was nearly as formidable as in his uniform.

"I'll drive you."

"There's no—" At his flat gray glance, she bit off the rest of the refusal. "Um...okay. Thank you."

For the next hour, she could hide in the bedroom, packing. That left only a short ride to her apartment. Ten minutes, perhaps fifteen. For that long a time she could hold back the tears and keep herself together. For fifteen minutes, maybe twenty. In the privacy of her own home she could let go—and she would worry afterwards about how to pick up the pieces.

Chapter Twelve

Stepping out of the squat brick library, Lila turned her face up to the fluffy flakes of snow drifting down over the street. The very first snowfall was magical in its ability to wash away the dingy-drab autumnal air of dead and dying things, the white drifts preparing the earth for change and rebirth.

The wind whipped her hair around her face and the soft snow into her eyes. But that was not the reason she had to blink.

Another winter. Another hockey season.

She'd learned not to turn on the television at half past the hour when the sports broadcasts all led off with talk of power play superiority and championship chances. It didn't matter that the championship series was six months away or that this first unseasonable snowfall would barely coat the roads, the city was hockey mad and last year's win made it hungry for another.

She averted her eyes from the figure of a teenager in a Toronto jersey. Most of the hockey jerseys she saw on the street nowadays carried Cahal's number and name emblazoned across the back. It was on his shoulders the city had battled its way to the number one spot atop the league and a trophy every Torontonian recognized.

She wondered what he had done with the trophy when it was his turn to take it. Every summer the members of the winning team took turns bringing the trophy home, taking pictures of it with their family, pretending to win it in street hockey tournaments, sleeping with it in their beds. The championship trophy went around Canada, to the hometowns of each individual player, and around the world to Russia, Sweden and the United States.

Lila's turn to touch the silver goal of every hockey player's heart would have to come with the rest of the public at the Hall of Fame, where the trophy usually stood during the regular season.

The excitement of the new season was impossible to avoid. Waiting for the bus, the team was on the lips of everyone in line and in her seat near the back, Lila could hear two elderly men talking excitedly about trade rumors. Lila had to smile. This early in the season, with the first few games of the year just under their belts, and the managers, coaches and players were already itching for change. Of course, Toronto was the last on that particular list; members of staff and the team itself would do anything to stay on with a winning team in the hopes of the same success repeating this year.

A familiar name stung her out of her listless contemplation of the advertisements.

"Cahal Wallace?" The second elderly man was repeating the name in stark disbelief. "What would he want a trade for? Doesn't he know when he's got a good team in front of him? Where else could he go and play with the same talent? Where could he get more money?"

Lila strained to hear his companion's response.

"I don't know that he wants more money or more talent."

"What then?" The second man was becoming quite angry with his companion, according him the usual treatment for a messenger.

"Personal reasons," was the first man's reply. "Rumor has it he wants a trade as far away as possible. I hear Montreal was interested but that wasn't far enough for him. Wallace is looking for a deal with Florida or Los Angeles."

"But why?" The question was plaintive.

A young man a couple of seats away leaned back to address the older men. "I heard it's because of his wife. You know, that little bitch that left him last year. He asked for a trade to Toronto to be near her and now that there's no chance between them, he wants out."

"That little bitch" flinched. Cahal wanted to get away, not just from her but also from the city that loved him. It was all her fault.

"Humph," the first old man said. "Isn't this city big enough for the two of them? Plenty of other people live in the same town as their ex-wife. Why can't he?"

"They were high school sweethearts," the young man explained. "You know, his one and only. When she left, it broke his heart."

"Hey," the young man's female companion exclaimed, "Cahal Wallace, isn't that the guy who was being stalked by that heiress? He's gorgeous! What woman in her right mind would walk out on him?"

Unable to hear anymore, Lila pulled the bell for the next stop and got out although it meant a slippery twelve-block hike to her apartment building.

In the safety of her apartment, it took her two hours to convince herself not to react unwisely to the news she'd just heard. It took the rest of the night to realize that she couldn't allow herself to do nothing.

*

At seven o'clock in the morning, three hours before her shift at the library was scheduled to begin, Lila was still groggy. Even so, she remembered her manners.

"Thank you for agreeing to see me, Billy."

The man seated across the table regarded her. "Don't thank me. I have a duty to follow my client's instructions."

"Cahal told you to see me?" Her question ended on a squeak of dismay.

An air of distasteful reluctance surrounded the sports agent. "Your husband gave me standing orders where you are concerned. Several times during the last year I have asked him to...confirm those directions."

She caught the hesitation. "You mean change them."

A quick frown marred the man's face.

"I say what I mean, Mrs. Wallace."

She had called him by his first name and the deliberate use of the formal means of address seemed to be his way of knocking her down a peg. Wrestling with her options, Lila decided to be direct.

"I've come about some rumors I've heard. Trade rumors."

Her rush of words was followed by a long pause.

Finally, he spoke. "They're more than rumors, Mrs. Wallace." From his desk, Billy Avery produced a thick pile of papers. In doing so, he dislodged several photographs sitting on his desk. "Those are the draft terms of a contract with the Los Angeles team."

But Lila was looking at one of the fallen photographs. It showed a blonde woman she recognized—from the photographs Chris had sent her. This was the woman who'd been in Cahal's hotel room at midnight.

"Who is that woman?"

"What?" Billy followed the direction of her gaze. "Oh, that's my associate, Carrie. She's also my daughter."

"Your daughter?"

The agent nodded happily as he passed her another photograph. "That's a more recent one of her and her family."

The photograph showed Carrie Jones, a pair of grinning children, and a tall handsome African-American man, all standing before the spreading ocean.

"She's based out of L.A.," Billy said. "Her husband's a basketball player there. I guess love of sport must run in the blood."

The room seemed to lose all of its air suddenly. Cahal had been telling the truth. That woman was a business contact and an employee of his agent. Everything she knew of Billy told her that his daughter would be just as respectable and upstanding as he was.

He put the pictures away then plucked the draft contract from her fingers.

"Once the details are hammered out, your husband will be on his way to California—at a substantially reduced salary."

"Reduced?" Lila repeated. After a winning season, it made no sense. If there had been any doubts about the matter before, Cahal had proven that he was the best goaltender in the league.

Billy Avery's eyes were sharp as he measured her reaction. "Your husband wants out of Toronto. At any price."

Glancing down at the papers, dotted in several places with pen marks, Lila said quickly, "But it's not a done deal, is it? Cahal hasn't signed anything."

"A formality," the agent dismissed, although his gaze was still measuring.

Lila placed unsteady fingers over the pile of sheets. "Do me a favor and don't send these off yet. I want to talk to him first."

The agent checked his wristwatch. "It's early yet so you might catch him at the practice arena."

She was already on her feet, snatching up her purse. "Thank you! I have to hurry."

As swiftly as she exited the office, she failed to see the wide grin that transformed Billy Avery's broad face.

*

At first glance, the arena appeared empty, the wide halls echoing only the sound of her hurried steps. Although few cars remained in the parking lot Lila had recognized the dark gray sedan, austere and powerful, its wealth understated in the same way Cahal was modest about his talents. The car stood out between an SUV and a low-slung sports car that screamed unnecessary expense.

Not daring to test the arena's security, she waited in the small alcove formed around the side entrance, watching parents and kids with figure skates slung around their shoulders stream in until she was convinced that she was waiting in the wrong place. Only her distant view of the dark gray car kept her from moving.

A tall figure walked by, carrying a long bag. Lila strained to see a face beneath the brim of a pulled down baseball cap. It wasn't him.

The man got into the sports car, leaping away in a burst of noise.

Lila shivered. She would give him one more minute.

Two minutes later, he pushed through the double doors, the action explosive. One of the doors bounced against the concrete wall outside and careened back. The other escaped hitting her.

"Watch out."

The raspy voice was flat and uncaring but even so the averted accident made him pause and she took advantage of the chance to say his name.

His swift downward glance revealed her face but his expression didn't change.

"Who're you waiting for?" The query was cool. "The only ones left back there are Efflin and Donovan."

Flushing, she took his point. Both players were married.

For some reason she was unable to say the most simple words: *I was waiting for you.*

"Billy told me that you were thinking about a trade." She didn't mention the photograph she'd seen of Carrie Jones. She couldn't. Not yet.

He pushed the bag behind him in an impatient gesture, making way for a harried looking woman with a set of twins in tow.

"It's more than just a thought at this point."

The low words made her stomach clench.

"I saw the contract," Lila said, not knowing what else to say. He looked so distant; the sole indication of his awareness of her was contained in the depths of his silvered eyes.

"Then you know all about it." Those piercing eyes moved away from her face. "The contract will be signed by the end of the week. I should be in L.A. by Monday."

Lila pushed a hand through her tangled hair and found it chilly and damp.

"Why? Why Los Angeles? Why at a reduced salary?"

A corner of his mouth moved upwards. "You are well informed."

"Cahal." His name was both protest and plea.

Looking around them, he said, "Not here. If you want to talk then I prefer to do it some place where we aren't risking illness."

"You never get sick," Lila said, moving to follow as he stepped out of the alcove.

Cool gray eyes rested on her sodden head. "I wasn't thinking of myself."

In the dark sedan he passed her a towel from his bag with a curt, "It's clean."

Feeling like a wayward child, Lila rubbed her hair vigorously; yet with slightly less wet locks she was still shivering.

Her husband drove in silence, fighting the rising tide of rush hour traffic with calm efficiency.

As he pulled in front of her building, she hesitated, not wanting to get out and lose the chance to speak to him.

"Can you come up?" Watching his impassive profile, she felt compelled to add, "Please?"

No part of him moved save for his lips. "I'll meet you up there."

She waited.

"Go on," he told her. "I have to park the car."

Dawdling, she watched his car disappear up the driveway, not believing he would be back. He buzzed her apartment five minutes later.

Cahal's eyes were busy upon entering her home, taking in the austere furnishings and vacant air. Spending most of her time at work, Lila had made no efforts to make the apartment cozier. Even before her sojourn in the penthouse, she had been disinclined to improve the generic unit.

When he looked at her, it was merely to say, "Why don't you go and change out of those wet clothes?"

He sounded even more reluctant to talk than ever.

Putting a hand up to her curling hair, Lila said, "I could do with a hot shower."

Perhaps she imagined the flicker in those silvery eyes.

"Don't let me keep you."

"I won't." Swallowing a heap of doubts, she walked to him. "I thought you might want to join me."

"What are you doing, Lila?" His voice was soft and devoid of anger.

Tilting her head back, she braced one hand against his chest. "Convincing you to stay in Toronto. With me."

He smiled at her but it was not with humor.

"You made it clear nearly a year ago that you weren't interested in living the life of a hockey player's wife. Why the sudden change of heart?"

She faltered and lowered her gaze. "Because I don't care about being the wife of a hockey player. I only want to be your wife."

He moved his hand up to trap her fingers against the front of his coat. "Which brings us back to my question, why the sudden change?"

With just hours to rehearse her speech, Lila hadn't done an adequate job. A dozen reasons came to her lips and she discarded each. She loved him, that was all that mattered. Yet she couldn't say so to cold gray eyes and that smiling mouth.

When she didn't answer, he tightened his hand.

"Do you know what I was doing in the weeks before you left me for the second time?"

Her normal voice was hiding in her throat and took a moment to coax out.

"No, Billy didn't fill me in to that extent."

He straightened his mouth into a hard line. "That's because, as with most things I do that concern you, my agent didn't approve."

Lila tried to smile. "It sounds important."

He moved his massive shoulders in a shrug. "That depends on who you talk to. I thought my retirement was pretty important. What fans I have would probably agree. You, of course, didn't care."

"Retire?" She sucked the word into her mouth, tasting it like a treat, before spitting out the first thing that came into her head. "You're barely thirty!"

"It's a tough sport," he pointed out. "Many players see their careers end prematurely because of injuries. A lot of players retire in their late twenties or early thirties and many of those who stay on do so past their prime. At the time I was thinking that it would be better to quit while I was still healthy and at the top of my game."

Lila felt dazed, as if she'd taken a body check from one of her husband's teammates.

"Quitting at the top," she mused. "It does have advantages. But it also has problems. The lack of a salary, for one."

Unlike his cousin, Cahal never pursued corporate endorsements throughout his career and after retirement offers would be hard to come by.

He looked down into her face, which was flushed and confused and, if she had known it, scared.

"That was why I was pursuing the next step, an alternate career." He nodded an acknowledgement of her wide-eyed stare. "Even the best hockey players retire by forty. That means another forty or so years of idleness. Few men could do that sentence."

Still he was saying nothing about the two of them, only his career, his retirement. Did he now see their futures as completely separate?

"W-what were you thinking of doing as a second career? Going back to school?"

His laughter was low and long. "It's a little late for that. No, what I was thinking of didn't require any better education than I've got at present. When you left last year I was in the final stages of working out a deal with the Real Sports station to be their number one anchorman."

Real Sports was the premier television sports station attracting a cultish following among young and middle-aged men, the exact demographic for which advertisers clamored. The station was based out of Toronto.

"That means—"

"That means I would stay in Toronto," he finished. "Permanently."

"And now?" Lila held her breath.

He leveled a sardonic look at her. "By now the position is no doubt filled by some other athlete seeking a ticket out of the cycle of injuries and championship derbies."

Ignoring the look, she pressed on. "But if they wanted a hockey player, you're by far the best choice. You're famous and at the peak of your game and you're just coming off of a championship win."

His mouth jerked out a smile. "Stop. You'll make my head swell."

Something in his voice made her pause.

"Cahal," she said, once she had digested the odd note, "you must know what I think of your abilities. You are a great player."

Dropping her hand, he moved several paces away. "Except you don't think what I do is that great."

"When have I ever said such a thing?"

His broad back told her nothing...and he wasn't talking, or even turning around to speak to her.

"Cahal, please, talk to me!"

The plea earned her a portion of his face in profile, the chiseled planes of cheek and jaw barely more articulate than his back, particularly since his eyes remained hidden.

"Don't be dense, Lila. You must remember your grandparents' views on my profession and no matter how much I tried to convince myself otherwise, I know you must agree with them to some degree."

"My grandparents' views?" She repeated his words. "My grandparents loved you!"

"Sure, just as much as they would have loved seeing their only grandchild marry a doctor or lawyer."

He believed what he was saying and realizing this Lila backed up and tried another tack.

"My grandparents are long gone. What could their views possibly have to do with us?"

He turned abruptly to face her. "They're your views too. You can't deny it."

"I do!" Lila shook her head. "You're crazy."

"Right. I'm only a hockey player."

"And I'm only a librarian," she shot back. "Do you know how strange people must find the fact that *you're* married to *me*?"

He lowered his dark gold lashes to shield the sudden glitter in his eyes. "They wouldn't find it strange if they met you."

"So why do you think I married you, in spite of my grandparents and your lack of education?"

The sizzling look grew cool as he refused to answer.

A long minute passed.

"Damn," Lila said. Bitter tears sprang to her eyes that she blinked back. "You must be even more cynical than your cousin. At least he's open with admitting he thinks money is everyone's motive."

"You would know all about it."

Unfair. "It was one night!"

"For all you know so was my...indiscretion."

That brought her up short. "Was it just one time?"

It would be in character for Chris to exaggerate a single lapse into a relentless pattern of infidelity.

Cahal's head moved from side to side. "No. It was zero."

The breath she hadn't been aware of holding back came out in a quick rush.

His eyes held hers. "You still haven't told me why you suffered this sudden change of heart? What made you want to be my wife again, if only for a crazy second?"

The crazy second was more like a few crazy days, ever since she heard those men on the bus talking about Cahal moving thousands of miles away. How could she explain that piercing stab of grief she felt at the thought of such a distance forever lying between them? How could she tell him that as long as he had lived in the city she had lived with the strangest notion that he was still bound to her, that any day now she might find him at her doorstep, ready with all of the sincere apologies and assurances she needed to give their relationship another chance?

"I-I didn't want to be alone again."

It was the first thing that came to her head and to say the truth would have been foolish and shameful. Then why did she feel so disappointed in herself?

"You won't be alone for long," Cahal predicted. "You'll make friends."

In two years, she hadn't made any lasting friendships. The friends she made in a day were lost in a day.

"Will I make husbands?"

The bitter question passed without comment. With his hands jammed into his pockets, Cahal seemed poised for flight. For once, there was no fight in that tall powerful body.

When she thought he would seize his chance to escape, he hesitated. What did he want, to impart one final civilized well-wishing comment? Lila felt that even a kind word would shred the last of her self-control.

"What did Chris tell you on the night of the charity ball?"

She met his gaze. He already knew the story. Was he just trying to torture her?

"Does it really matter?"

His silence was unhelpful.

Blowing out a breath, she said, "Fine. He told me about the night we spent together. Or should I say, the night we supposedly spent together?"

"What about that night?"

Lila stared up at him. As much as she stared, she couldn't see into his thoughts. Would it help to finally tell him the truth or would it just hurt him more?

She groped for the wall and leaned against it, resting her hip against the cool plaster. In her damp clothes, she felt awkward and clumsy and with her hair wild on her head she knew she must look like a character from Macbeth.

"I could never remember exactly what happened that night," she explained. "One minute Chris and I were sitting in the living room sharing a bottle of wine and then next minute I'm waking up in bed. I vaguely remember Chris carrying me upstairs but that's all. It was Chris who told me what happened."

"Of course," her husband gritted out, his voice still emotionless. "What did he tell you?"

She kept her gaze on the floor. Puddles of water marred the cheap tile.

"That we had sex, twice, and we showered together before falling asleep." Lila shuddered, the memory of the lie still powerful.

Cahal's voice was very low. "Isn't that what happened?"

"No." Her face was suddenly damp again. "He lied. He told me at the ball. He lied about having sex. He lied about the shower we took together. He lied about everything."

A long silence seemed to swell to fill the room, cold and ugly.

"So he didn't rape an unconscious woman," Cahal said. "Instead he pretended to rape an amnesiac one."

Lila's eyes lifted as far as his chest. "I wasn't amnesic. I had too much to drink, that's all."

"Wine?" He sounded scathing. "You couldn't pass out if you downed an entire bottle of that weak stuff we used to keep in the house, much less if you shared it with someone like my cousin. Are you sure he didn't slip something into your glass?"

She shifted her gaze another few inches upwards. It was true that she wasn't much of a drinker and she attributed the blackout to her emotional state. Now she wasn't quite so sure.

Cahal was more certain.

A quick peek revealed her husband's face to be very grim.

"He knew you were alone and upset and he invited himself over in the middle of the night. I'm sure he came prepared. The premeditated use of an intoxicating substance makes the difference between a vicious charade and a serious crime. Chris was always pretty good at skirting the line. He must have really enjoyed giving that statement to my lawyer. I should have realized something was up from the way he refused to swear it under oath."

"He did a lot of damage," Lila agreed.

Cahal was less oblique. "He did what he set out to do and that was to destroy our marriage."

She swiveled her brown eyes upwards. "Only if we let him."

He turned away and her gaze was left fixed on the spot he'd occupied. It was too late for the truth. Too late for everything.

A raspy voice came from over his shoulder. "Do you know what I sent him to explain to you at the ball?"

"I-it wasn't about what happened between me and him that night?"

He shook his head. "No, I just learned about that a moment ago when you told me. My cousin kept that information up his sleeve."

With a keen sensation of futility, Lila made herself ask, "What is it then?"

Instead of answering, he pulled a cell phone out of an inner pocket and began punching in numbers on its face. The small device was smaller in his big hand and its appearance had the sudden conjure of a magic trick. If only he could produce something magical from that same pocket, something to make everything all right.

After a few seconds, he handed her the phone. "It's better you hear it directly from the source."

The recorded voice at her ear told her that there was one saved message, nearly a year old. She pressed another button to hear it.

Cahal. It's me.

The sound of the familiar masculine voice brought her eyes up to her husband. His expression was unenlightening.

The next part of the recording was more cocky, less hesitant. It became what Lila had always thought of as quintessentially Chris Wallace.

I did what you wanted, cousin. I told her the truth tonight. A slight pause. *I told Lila that I lied about the women and the cheating. I told her she could ask anyone in the league and anyone would tell her that you were the most faithful husband in the sport.* Another pause. *I think she believed me. Hope you get your happy ending.* Click.

Lila handed the phone back and she watched her husband shut it off with a decisive movement.

"I've carried that around for the past year."

The raspy voice was nearly inaudible.

"Oh my God."

Lila spun away, her hands feeling for the wall and following it into the living room where she collapsed onto the small sofa.

Cahal followed. "You didn't know, did you?"

She shook her head. Two years ago, she'd been so ready to believe Chris and just a year ago, in her insecurity, she'd accepted the lie again even though Chris admitted to lying about something just as important.

Cahal would never forgive her. She didn't think anybody short of a saint could pardon such a betrayal.

"Why did he do it?"

A ghost of a smile played over his hard mouth. "The same reason he sabotaged my equipment when our teams played each other for the junior league championship. The same reason he crashed the motorbike I got for my birthday. The same reason he lied about sleeping with you. He wanted something I had or I wanted and he couldn't stand to see me with it."

Lila knew about the motorbike but not the junior league championship. The pattern was evident, yet her sympathy had gone to the wrongdoer.

"You make him sound like a monster."

With a widening smile, he reclaimed her hand, halting its frenetic twisting. "He's not a monster, darling, any more than Victoria was. He's a man who never learned to deal with his jealousy in a straightforward way and let it take control of his life."

She watched his hand envelop hers. "I know now that you were telling the truth about the woman in your hotel room. Why didn't you tell me it was Billy's daughter?"

"Would it have made a difference?"

No, perhaps not. She'd been so hurt, so blind, for so long. She'd been so very stupid.

Her fingers fluttered against his palm. "I love you, Cahal."

"Nice time to remember it."

A dent appeared to soften the harsh planes of his cheek and her free hand traced it.

"I never forgot it. Not for a single minute."

At the slight pressure of her grasp, he lowered his head until their foreheads touched. "Is that why you came to me today, in spite of what you thought I did?"

It was a difficult thing to admit, to let go of her pride.

"Yes."

"Baby." His voice altered, becoming warm and low. "I love you so much. I would never look at another woman, much less love one."

She asked him, "Why couldn't you have convinced me of that two years ago?"

"I tried, if you remember. I was boxing shadows. I wasn't sure about the identity of your source of information. If I'd known that it was my cousin all along..." Breaking off, he swallowed before he continued. "I suspected something was up with him but I wanted you to trust me and I couldn't believe that you would accept anything he told you."

Lila moved her hand from his face. "I should have trusted you. I-I'm sorry."

"Don't apologize," he told her. "I was wrong, too. Against my better judgment, I believed some of things my cousin told me. I started to see how you could be ashamed of me. After we separated, the life you chose was so different, as if you were rejecting everything we shared together."

"I was never ashamed of you," Lila said. "I thought you were unsatisfied with me. I'm not a former model or gymnast. I'm nothing special."

"Aren't you?" her husband asked before crushing his mouth to hers.

The kiss was devouring, fierce with the pent-up longing of the past year and the need for unity long teased out but ultimately denied. When he lifted his fair head, Cahal was breathing hard and Lila experienced a sharp stab of pleasure

"You are so special, my darling. You're my wife and the only woman I've ever loved."

Lila's eyes misted. He'd never been vocal with his declarations and this choked rasp was heavy with the depth of his feelings. His hand shook as he caressed the length of her arm.

"Then why didn't you want to have children?"

He stopped moving his hand as a long pause turned into a longer silence.

"Cahal?"

He took a deep breath. "The truth is, Lila, that I was selfish. I had so little time with you during the season that I wanted every minute to myself and I knew that a child would divide even that time by at least half."

"And now?"

After asking the question, she held her own breath.

He smiled. "And now that my retirement from hockey is right around the corner I think we might want something small and cute to fill our time."

Hitting his shoulder, she said, "You'd better not be talking about getting a puppy."

Threading his fingers through her dark hair, he kissed her again.

"No, darling, I'm thinking about a baby for us to share our love with."

But Lila was realistic. "That would be lovely," she said, "but I would be happy either way, sharing my love with you."

Cahal hauled her closer for a long hard kiss.

About the Author

Nan Comargue writes contemporary and erotic romance. She lives in Toronto, Canada and has been reading romance novels since she could read. She blogs at *http://nancomargue.blogspot.ca/* and can be found on Twitter at @NanComargue.

In the mood for more Crimson Romance? Check out *The Marrying Kind* by Judith Anne McCarthy at *CrimsonRomance.com*.

www.ingramcontent.com/pod-product-compliance
Lightning Source LLC
Chambersburg PA
CBHW010639100726
47900CB00011B/2901